THE SORROW

This book is a work of fi

Names, characters, organisations, places, events and incidents are either products of the author's imagination or are used fictitiously.

All rights reserved.

No part of this book may be reproduced or stored in a retrieval system or transmitted in any form or by any means, electronic, mechanical, photocopying, recording or otherwise without express permission from the author.

C J Galtrey.

John Gammon Peak District Detective

Book five, series two of the John Gammon Peak District Detective.

John is about to commit to a different life, little does he know of the twists and turns that will affect him in this Christmas blockbuster.

While writing this book I had quite a serious car accident. I would like to thank everyone who took the time to message me with best wishes. A really big thank you to my sister and brother-in-law for the amount of running about they have done for me. So a big thank you to Linda and Ben Hancock, two of the most incredible people in my life.

THE SORROW BEGINS

This is the tenth book over two series of our detective John Gammon. Below are all the books available on Amazon in Paperback and Kindle format.

SERIES ONE

BOOK ONE: '**Things will never be the same again**'.

BOOK TWO: '**Sad Man**'.

BOOK THREE: '**Joy Follows Sorrow**'.

BOOK FOUR: '**Never cry on a bluebell**'.

BOOK FIVE: '**Annie Tanney**'.

John Gammon Peak District Detective

SERIES TWO

BOOK ONE: '**The poet and the calling card**'.

BOOK TWO: '**Why**'.

BOOK THREE: '**Your past is your future**'.

BOOK FOUR: '**Intravenous**'.

BOOK FIVE: '**The sorrow begins**'.

THE SORROW BEGINS

Below are other books not from the John Gammon series.

<u>THE TRILOGY</u>

It all starts with Liam Egan and his dreams which carry on with his daughter in The Hurt of Yochana, and finally his grandson in Grove

BOOK ONE: '**Looking for Shona**'.

BOOK TWO: '**The hurt of Yochana**'.

BOOK THREE: '**Grove**'.

John Gammon Peak District Detective

TWO ONE-OFF BOOKS

'Got to Keep Running': Saskia Wagers is very successful in her banking career until that fateful day. Follow Saskia from London to Cornwall eventually ending up in the Peak District. Live Saskia's dreams and prayers that this may end one day.

'I am Fawn Jones': A thriller set in Jersey and Dorset. Three girls go missing presumed by their families who are close that the girls have run away to the mainland. All their thoughts begin to change when an eccentric man contacts them.

THE SORROW BEGINS

Contents

CHAPTER ONE 8

CHAPTER TWO 46

CHAPTER THREE 88

CHAPTER FOUR 125

CHAPTER FIVE 168

CHAPTER SIX 203

CHAPTER SEVEN 242

CHAPTER NINE 320

CHAPTER TEN 358

CHAPTER ELEVEN 403

John Gammon Peak District Detective

CHAPTER ONE

John and Sandra stood on the old former railway bridge in the dark and reeled at the realisation that the person that was going to blackmail John was a friend.

"Carol what the hell are you doing?"

They helped her to her feet. She was shaking and crying.

"John, I am so sorry," Carol repeated this a few times.

"Just calm down Carol, let's sit down and talk this out."

"Why would you want to blackmail me?"

The three of them sat on the small wooden bench that had been put there for walkers to enjoy the spectacular view.

THE SORROW BEGINS

The inscribed words on the seat seemed even more ironic 'The Greatest Gift of Life is Friendship' it said.

Carol was crying; upset yes, but also the pepper spray administered by Scooper was stinging her eyes.
In between crying and blowing her nose Carol Lestar started to tell John her story that led to the situation she now found herself in.

"Sixteen months ago Mum became poorly. We were backwards and forwards to the doctors and the hospital. Then three month ago we were given the earth-shattering news that Mum had Systemic Lupus Erythematosus to give it its full name. Mum hasn't been good, and it is

John Gammon Peak District Detective

affecting her kidneys and they think her brain."

"I saw your Mum the other week Carol, she looked fine."

"Yes John, there are times when it is in remission but then times when it's horrendous for her. They have told us that it will only get worse and there is no cure. We came home after receiving the diagnosis and just sat and cried. Me and mum go everywhere together, holidays everything. I am not a person to give up, so I spent night after night on the internet looking for a ray of hope. Four weeks ago I found it. In America there is a surgeon in Falstaff, Arizona that claims he can slow the onset of the disease by eighty five percent, but at a cost. I worked it all out and the bill was

THE SORROW BEGINS

twenty eight thousand pounds. I have about eight thousand saved up for a rainy day but that left me twenty thousand pounds short. I was desperate John."

"Carol, you have known me since I was a little boy, why didn't you just ask?"

"Pride I guess John. Look where my pride has got me now. I intended to pay you back anonymously once the cleaning business takes off. John I am so sorry, please believe that. What was I thinking of?"

"Carol, you are a friend, you know I have been left large amounts of money over the years. Do you think I would see you or your Mum stuck if there is a chance I could help?"

Carol was too upset to answer.

John Gammon Peak District Detective

"Look Carol, meet me Monday night at the Spinning Jenny and I will sort this out for you. Bring your bank details."

Carol finished crying.

"I don't know what to say."

"And don't worry, it won't go any further, will it Sandra?"

"Of course not, you have no worries on that score Carol from me."

John laughed, "I have to ask you one thing though Carol, where did you get the trial bike from?"

"I borrowed it off Jimmy Lowcee. I told him I wanted to get fit so he loaned it me for a week. I nearly fell off it coming here."

THE SORROW BEGINS

Both Sandra and John were in stitches. John was feeling relieved in a strange sense that it was Carol who was the extortionist, in fact it did make him smile a bit.

"Sorry about the pepper spray Carol."

"You were only doing your job Sandra. Please never repeat this will you?"

"Of course not, my word is my bond."

"Thanks Sandra."

"Ok now, go careful Carol and I will see you Monday night."

"I don't know what to say John."

Carol got on the mountain bike and wobbled of down the track.

"John, that was so sweet of you. That's what I like about you," and she kissed him.

John Gammon Peak District Detective

The spark between these two had never gone away.

"Now what?" Sandra said.

"Have you got to get back for Rosie?"

"No Mum has taken her to see her friend in Bournemouth on one of those bus trips that Slicks from Micklock do."

"Well if that's the case you could stay at mine tonight if you want?"

"I was planning on it, Mr Gammon," and she tweaked his bottom as they made their way back to the cars.

It was 10.10pm when John and Sandra arrived back at John's cottage.

"I have got some champagne in the fridge Sandra, do you fancy that?"

THE SORROW BEGINS

"Super John, just need to freshen up so will see you upstairs."

John caught a glimpse of Sandra's long legs disappearing up the oak staircase. He poured two glasses and put the bottle in an ice bucket. He placed the champagne on the bedside cabinet undressed and climbed into bed eagerly awaiting Sandra. The bedroom door opened and he wasn't disappointed. Sandra had a light blue basque with light blue stockings and black high heels. Her dark hair tumbled over her smooth white china like shoulders.

"Don't move Mr Gammon, my turn first," she said. "Lay back and enjoy."

John's heart was racing. Sandra looked incredibly sexy and she began by kissing

John Gammon Peak District Detective

him everywhere. She told John to hold the rustic bed head with each hand and he wasn't allowed to touch her. She started by passionately kissing him then progressed down his body. John felt like his whole body would explode. She teased him for almost twenty minutes before telling him to take all of her. John willingly obliged, this was uncontrollable lust from both of them. Sandra was screaming with emotion. When it was finally over they lay back both covered in beads of sweat. Sandra passed John a glass of champagne. John looked at her. If ever there was a reason to call off his engagement it was tonight.

"Sandra, I really don't know what to do about tomorrow."

THE SORROW BEGINS

"I can't decide for you John, but I am not sure you love her enough to be honest."

"Think I will sleep on it."

Sandra laid her head on John's chest and they both fell sound asleep.

The following morning John could smell bacon cooking, Sandra was up and about. He was about to get up when his mobile rang. It was Saron.

"Hi sweetie," she said, "Shall I come down for some breakfast?"

John had to think quickly.

"Ugh, no Saron, I am just nipping into work. I had a development on Clive Wiggledon."

"Don't be late this afternoon will you John?"

"Of course not, but just need to nip into work, should only be a couple of hours."

John Gammon Peak District Detective

"Ok see you at Mum's. Be there for 2.00pm please."

"I will," and the phone went dead.

John went down to Sandra who had now made the bacon sandwiches. She was standing in one of John's shirt and nothing else.

"Guessing that was Saron. So, what are you going to do stud muffin?"

"I can't let her down and it's not like we will be married. If I find I feel like this in a couple of months I can always call it a day."

"Mr Gammon you are naughty."

"Not as naughty as you Miss Scooper, leading me astray," and they both laughed.

"So, are you coming this afternoon?"

THE SORROW BEGINS

"Don't think so John, even I am not that brazen."

John was a bit relieved but didn't want to show it. Scooper left, and John got himself ready for the engagement party.

He arrived at 2.00pm and found the whole of the village had been decorated with bunting. On the big gates at the entrance of the drive to Trissington Hall were banners saying 'Congratulations Saron and John'. John really didn't want all this fuss. Saron came straight over as he got out of the car. She had a lilac two-piece suit similar the type Jackie Onassis made famous in the sixties, she really did look stunning. His mind wandered back to Tracey Rodgers and Sandra Scooper. What the hell is wrong with me he thought. He settled his mind that it was kind of a last fling and that's how he tried to justify it to himself.

"John, come on we have to mingle with everyone."

The scene was set like something you read about in OK magazine. Lady Jervis had arranged for a top London photographer to take pictures of the day. It was then that Saron said the pictures would go in the high society magazine Tatler. John was a bit shocked.

"Don't they have royalty pictures in there?"

THE SORROW BEGINS

"Are you forgetting John, we are distant cousins of the Queen of England?"

This all hit John. The reality was Saron's mother was a Lady and his mum and dad had been farmers!

The afternoon went quite well. Saron seemed very happy and everyone commented on how pretty she looked. John felt a nice glow knowing she was on his arm and he decided this was it. He would commit no more dalliances to Saron and hope she never found out about previous the ones. Lord and Lady Cote Heath offered them a week in Aruba. Apparently they had a three bedroomed house right on the beach. Saron's mum said before Lord Jervis died they often went twice a year.

John Gammon Peak District Detective

"What do you reckon John? If I can sort some cover at the pub, could you get a week off?"

"I suppose so."

"Well don't get too enthusiastic, will you?"

"Sorry sweetheart, I would just like to get Wiggledon put away then we could go."

"There is more to life than the police force John."

She knew as soon as she said it she shouldn't have. John's job was his life.

It was soon Monday morning and work again. The drive in was enjoyable. It was a touch frosty in the fields and John could feel the beginnings of winter coming on. He arrived at Bixton and checked with Sergeant Yap if there had been any

THE SORROW BEGINS

developments on Clive Wiggledon, but he had nothing new to report.

"Thanks Sergeant. Is DCI Cook in yet?"

"Sorry Sir, I was just about to say she called a couple of minutes ago for you and asked you call her back."

"Ok Ian."

Gammon went to his office and called DCI Cook.

"Hi John, I got a call from Gareth Cawley the Home Secretary's PA last night. He said the Home Secretary, Sir Nicholas Banks, wants a meeting with me in Oxford at the Three Swans Hotel. I don't think it's anything un-toward but he will be asking for updates. At the moment only clean up is required for the arrest of Clive Wiggledon,

John Gammon Peak District Detective

so if you can make sure the team are focusing on that please."

"Will do Amanda."

"Anything else happened, John?"

"Not at the moment, all is quiet on the western front as they say."

"Ok John, well I will see you tomorrow afternoon. Oh, and thanks for a great party at Trissington Hall. I thoroughly enjoyed it. You are a lucky man, she is a very pretty girl."

Gammon set about his paperwork with gusto. He knew he had loads of reports to catch up on so needed to get disciplined. It was 2.40pm when Gammon looked up from his pile of reports. He was just about to get a cup of the famed station coffee when Yap

THE SORROW BEGINS

called to say a lady was in reception and would like to see him. Gammon made his way down to the front desk. A very well-dressed lady with a posh accent introduced herself.

"Pamela Mule, and you are?" she said.

"Detective Inspector Gammon."

"I am honored DI Gammon, you are the famous detective."

Gammon didn't like her snobbish attitude.

"How can we help you?"

"Do we have somewhere we could talk privately?"

"Sergeant Yap," Gammon said, "I will be in interview room one should you need me."

"Would you like a coffee?"

John Gammon Peak District Detective

"No, I would never drink that American muck, I will have a tea. Please ensure it is in a china cup young man," she said to Sergeant Yap.

Got a bloody beauty here, Yap thought.

Once in the room, Gammon questioned Pamela Mule.

"What is this about? Do you mind if I call you Pamela?"

"By all means, Mr Gammon."

"Ok Pamela, so please explain the problem."

"Well it's Duncan you see."

"That's Mr Mule?"

"Yes, my husband you must have heard of him?"

THE SORROW BEGINS

"I'm sorry why would I know your husband?"

"He was five times Formula One Champion during the eighties."

Gammon knew straight away who he was, but he wasn't giving her the pleasure.

"Sorry Pamela I don't have a lot of time for sport."

"Anyway, he went golfing two days ago with some chums. Apparently when he left the clubhouse he was quite the worse for wear and he hasn't been seen since."

"Does he ever stay away from home? I am wondering why it wasn't reported the night of his disappearance?"

"I only got back from St Moritz this morning. When Duncan wasn't there I called Freddie."

"Freddie?"

John Gammon Peak District Detective

"Yes Freddie Slack, they are good friends. His wife does a lot of charity work with me for the local hospital."

"What did Mr Slack say?"

"Well it was Sondra his wife who answered. She said Freddie was golfing as always. But she said Freddie was surprised that my Duncan hadn't phoned. But he did say Duncan was probably in the dog house after getting so drunk the other night. I am very worried Mr Gammon."

"There may be a reasonable explanation. Can you tell me who he would have played golf with?"

"Well Freddie Slack of course, then there would have been Roger Thorndyke, Alec Bent, Ollie Wilkins and Bobby Lint."

THE SORROW BEGINS

"So, these are the guys he always plays golf with."

"Yes, they have holidays together also. They are all retired successful business men so as they say birds of a feather."

"Ok, write down your address Mrs Mule. Here is my card and we will start investigations right away."

"That's very good of you Mr Gammon. Next time I see Sir Nicholas Banks I will mention your prompt attention."

This made Gammon smile, she just had to name drop didn't she. Pamela Mule left the station and Gammon called out Sergeant Magic to come along to Bixton Golf Club to see if they could talk with these guys.

John Gammon Peak District Detective

Bixton Golf Club was a premier club in the area, with a waiting list for membership that currently stood at ten years. The green fees and membership alone were astronomical, so only the rich played here. Over the years the place had been developed. The old club house frontage was kept and integrated into the new buildings. As they pulled up a green keeper wandered over.

"You can't park there, this is for members only."

Gammon flashed his warrant card.

"I don't care if you were Lord or Lady Jervis, you still can't park there."

The reference made Gammon smile and he nudged Magic not to say anything.

THE SORROW BEGINS

"So, where would you like us to park then?"

"Go down there and round the back of the clubhouse, you can park there. Can I just say, if you have the need to call again please ensure you park where I have instructed you," and he marched off.

"Well that's us told Magic."

"Silly man," said Magic.

As Gammon and Magic entered the clubhouse it went a little quiet. There were three older guys sitting at a table and five blokes at the bar. It all appeared very stuffy. Gammon approached the bar where a very pretty girl was working.

"Can I help gentlemen?"

Gammon and Magic showed their warrant cards. The girl was wearing denim hot pants and a tight low-cut top. The guys

John Gammon Peak District Detective

at the bar were just ogling and being suggestive but Gammon guessed she dressed for the tips.

"I am looking to speak with some gentlemen that are friends with Duncan Mule."

"What has the old fool done now? Has she thrown him out?" and the guy laughed.

"And you are Sir?"

"Freddie Slack."

"Oh Mr Slack, you are one of the people his wife mentioned he was with the night he disappeared."

"Well yes, me and some others, in fact us lot, hey lads."

"Ok so can I take some names please?"

A small balding guy stood up.

"Alec Blake."

THE SORROW BEGINS

The next one, a tall man with a moustache that was jet black, only his hair was silver grey said, "Roger Thorndyke."

"Ollie Wilkins," said the man who was quite a bit younger than the others. Gammon thought maybe he was late forties, he had receding ginger hair and was about six foot tall. Finally the next guy said his name was Bobby Lint. He was early fifties but looked like he worked out, maybe ex-army Gammon thought. He had a close-cropped haircut and was about five feet ten.

"Ok gentlemen, if you could give Sergeant Magic here your contact numbers and addresses should we need to contact you further."

While Magic was taking details, he took the chance to speak with the bar person.

John Gammon Peak District Detective

"What's your name?"

"Iman Oglee."

"Were you working the night Mr Mule was last seen?"

She hesitated a little which concerned Gammon.

"I was on until 9.00pm but then I left."

"Who took over from you then?"

"Maggie Silito, she is the bar manager."

"Do you have an address for Mrs. Silito?"

"Oh, she isn't married."

"Ok then Miss Silito."

"Somewhere in my handbag."

"Ok when my Sergeant finishes collecting these addresses please give him yours and Miss Silito's and your contact numbers please."

THE SORROW BEGINS

With all this done Gammon said thank you and emphasized that Mr Mule may well turn up, but if not he would be questioning each of them at the station.

"Not a lot more we can do here Magic, you drive back so I can look at these addresses.

"Did any address stand out to you Sergeant Magic?"

"I copped the girl in the hot pants address."

"No you plonker, think like a detective for once in your life!"

"Sorry Sir, no not really, why?"

"Well the one that stands out is Bobby Lint. He doesn't appear to be from their crowd and he lives on the council estate in south Dilley Dale."

John Gammon Peak District Detective

"Maybe just a coincidence Sir."

"Oh, just get me back to the station Magic."

Magic quite often wound his colleagues up with his lack of common sense.

"Anything happening Sergeant Yap?"

"Nothing at work Sir, but Derby have just sacked their manager."

"Oh wippee dee do," Gammon said as he climbed the stairs to his office.

Football wasn't his favourite sport. He met DI Scooper at the top of the stairs.

"How did the engagement party go then?"

"Yes, it was a nice afternoon."

"Does that mean the end of our dalliance?"

THE SORROW BEGINS

"Come into my office Sandra."

Sandra sat down and John took his coat off and sat across from her.

"I have to try and make this work Sandra, for everyone's sake."

"Not for mine John. We are good together you know that, or you wouldn't keep coming back each time."

"Look I know what it seems like."

"What, like you have used me again?"

"Come on Sandra it wasn't like that and you know it."

"Look this conversation is done," and Sandra flounced out of Gammon's office.

They had a lot of history together, and a baby they should have had, other than the hatred Whisky Grant had for John. He knew when he was with Sandra she was special to him. Equally Saron held that something special, but he had decided to commit to Saron, so he had to get on with it. Just then the phone rang it was Saron.

"Hey John, great news I have a new business partner."

"That's great news, who is it?"

"It's a guy called Jamie Mixom. He's from Stockport, great guy run pubs before, and been successful. He wanted to move into the country so it's a perfect fit, plus he is fit," and she laughed. "Come up tonight and I will introduce you. He is doing the 6.00pm – close shift. He really is keen John."

"Ok well at least we might get some time together now."

"I am sure we will once Jamie has settled in. He can cook as well."

THE SORROW BEGINS

"Sounds like a guy of many talents then," John said sarcastically.

"Put the green-eyed monster away Gammon and get yourself up here tonight."

Gammon decided to have the friends of Duncan Mule interviewed formally the next day, and he arranged with DI Milton and Sergeant Magic to get that arranged. It was now 4.30pm and time to go and meet Saron's new business partner, much as he really wasn't interested but thought he best.

John arrived at the Tow'd Man and could see Saron chatting with a guy at the bar.

"Hey John. This is my fiancé Jamie."

John Gammon Peak District Detective

Jamie Mixom introduced himself. He looked like something off that Love Island program everyone raves about. He was about six feet with dark hair shaved at the sides and greased on top. His teeth were so white they dazzled you. He had a tattoo sleeve depicting a dragon. His shirt looked like it was two sizes too small and his trouser were so tight they looked like they had been sprayed on. What the hell was Saron thinking John thought?

"So, a policeman, eh John?"

"Yes, that's correct Jamie."

"Upholding the law in the sticks eh?"

John felt this was a swipe at his ambition.

"John is quite famous, Jamie. He is an expert in serial killers."

THE SORROW BEGINS

"Best not introduce him to some of my friends from Manchester," and he laughed. His laugh even grated on John.

"So, who's killing who here in Emmerjail?" and he laughed at his silly reference to Emmerdale but with jail. Again John could feel the cringe worthiness of the man. Saron said she best get in the kitchen so John followed her.

"What the hell have you done?"

"What do you mean John?"

"I mean that bloody moron, have you signed anything?"

"No, we have arranged for the solicitor to have the papers ready to sign next week."

"Well I suggest you rethink Saron."

"Not jealous are we John?"

John Gammon Peak District Detective

"What, over that excuse for a man? Definitely not but what I do know is he will ruin your business."

"Look I am too busy to talk now, we can talk later."

"Tell you what, I'm going for a beer, so I will see you tomorrow," and John petulantly left Saron open-mouthed at the grill.

He arrived at the Spinning Jenny feeling in a real argumentative mood.

"Hiya John, what can I get you?"

"Pedigree Kev please."

"Somebody sounds in a grump? You two haven't fallen out already have you? That would be a record even for you John lad."

THE SORROW BEGINS

"Saron just took on a business partner and I can see that he will be a disaster."

"Not good then mate?"

"Absolutely not Kev."

Kev gave John his pint then started serving at the other end of the bar. Carol Lestar arrived, she looked sheepishly at John.

"Why weren't you at the engagement party Carol?"

"I am so embarrassed John. How could I go to that after what I did?"

"Don't be soft now, have you got your bank details and I will sort the transfer in the morning?"

"John, I have had time to sleep on it, and I can't take your money. I told Mum and she wasn't best pleased."

John Gammon Peak District Detective

"Look, neither of you have a choice. If I can give your Mum some quality of life then I will. I would never forgive myself if I didn't."

John shouted across to Kev. "Is it ok if a use a piece of your food order book Kev?"

"No problem mate."

John instructed Carol to write down her bank details, then he bought her a double vodka and skinny coke. Carol pecked him on the cheek.

"I owe you big time John, thank you so much. You don't know how much of a worry it's been."

"I can imagine, now forget what happened, it's all turned out good in the

THE SORROW BEGINS

end. Just one thing, did you give Jimmy his bike back?"

"He wasn't too pleased, I buckled the front wheel taking it back to him."

"That's some kind of omen Carol."

"What do you mean John?"

"I mean somebody is telling you not to go bike riding," and he laughed.

"You are a good friend John, you really are."

"Hey, you have always been there for me when I lost Mum, Dad and Adam, so it's the least I can do."

Carol drank her drink thanked John again and left him with his thoughts.

John Gammon Peak District Detective

CHAPTER TWO

About 9.10pm Bob and Jack arrived.

"Best get the boys a drink."

"Where have you two renegades been?"

"Only just turned out, the girls are at Badminton. Bob say's its all whites and Barley Water."

"I knew you would have a name for it Bob."

Just then the door opened and the girls arrived. Cheryl, Shelley, Sheba, Tracey Rodgers and a friend of Sheba's who John hadn't met before. Jack got the girls a drink and Sheba and her friend stood talking to John.

THE SORROW BEGINS

"This is my friend Linda Sterndale. She lives in Hittington married to Phil the builder."

"Pleased to meet you Linda. How long have you two been mates?"

"Ever since me and Phil moved into the village. I quite like sheep so me and Sheba hit it off straight away."

"Linda has won best Premier Cake of the show for the last eight years at Hittington John. She is to shy to admit it, but her cakes are divine."

"What did you win this year?"

"Well the Premier Class is for cake makers that can make cakes that are not your usual Victoria Sponge type. This year I won with my Tipsy Mallow Cake."

"Sounds lovely, what did it consist of?"

John Gammon Peak District Detective

"Well the sponge is mixed with Guinness. Then I split the cake and fill the centre with raspberry jam. On the top I mixed marsh mallow with Amaretto and finished it off with chunks of white chocolate."

"Blimey that sounds lovely."

Linda blushed.

"So, what has Mr Gammon been up to, other than getting engaged to the lovely Saron?"

John could detect Sheba's sarcasm.

"Not a lot to be honest, work is quite steady at the minute."

They all went and sat down chatting until almost 11.00pm and John decided to call it a day. On the way back to the cottage

THE SORROW BEGINS

John had a thought so he rang the station. Sergeant Di Trimble answered.

"Good evening Di."

"Oh, good evening Sir, how can I help you?"

"I told Magic to arrange for the golf club lot to be bought in for questioning, but I have had second thoughts. The other DI's can handle that. Tell DI Milton to see me at 9.00am please."

"Will do Sir."

"Everything else ok Di?"

"Yeah quiet tonight Sir."

"Ok thank you," and John rang off.

Gammon was in early the next day, well early for him, 8.30am. He needed to make a start on the paperwork. He could see DCI Cook was already in, so he put his head round the door.

"Good morning Amanda."

"Oh, hi John."

"How did your meeting go with Sir Nicholas Banks?"

"Yes, quite good. He wined and dined me on his expenses of course."

"So, what did he want?"

"He basically wanted an update on the Clive Wiggledon case. From what I could get out of him MI6 have been trying to find this guy for a few years."

"Why what had he done?"

"The list was as long as my arm, John. Illegal arms sales to Libya, moving drugs through Indonesia with drug mules. Laundering money and his big one. Can

THE SORROW BEGINS

you remember the case about four years ago when the Balidon diamond was stolen from the diamond display at Earls Court?"

"Yeah remember that, but they didn't find out for a year because whoever nicked it replaced it with an exact copy."

"Yes, that's right John, and they would never have known but it went on tour round Europe so had to be reassessed for insurance purposes, and that's when they found it was a fake. It shook the diamond industry to the core."

"So, they think Wiggledon was involved?"

"It's believed he masterminded it."

"So why would he come back here doing a poxy job, then killing all these people."

John Gammon Peak District Detective

"He believed he was untouchable, guess he didn't figure on John Gammon, did he John?"

"Nice of you to say so Amanda, but it was a team effort."

"Credit where it's due John that's my motto. So, anything new while I was away?"

John told her about Duncan Mule's supposed disappearance.

"Well it's certainly nice to be a bit quieter eh, John? Now that Interpol, MI6 and MI5 are looking for Wiggledon it makes our lives easier."

John didn't really agree so he said nothing. He wanted to collar Wiggledon for Bixton police not flippin' MI6 or whoever.

THE SORROW BEGINS

"Right I best get on Amanda. I am going to have a look at where these people from the golf club live."

"Ok see you later John."

Gammon had given up on doing any paperwork so he arranged for DI Scooper and DI Lee to question Freddie Slack and Alec Blake. Di Smarty and Sergeant Magic would question Roger Thorndyke and Ollie Wilkins. That left Bobby Lint, Iman Oglee and Maggie Silito. They were to report back the following morning at a meeting in the incident room. Gammon and Milton set off for Bobby Lint's place. On the way Carl asked John a strange question.

"Do you believe in miracles?"

"I'm not sure Carl, why do you ask?"

John Gammon Peak District Detective

"Look, you are going to think I am nuts, but I was out walking near Snowerton Lane, you know about three miles out of Dilley Dale. I have just had a new dog called Crisp."

"Strange name for a dog."

"It's not John. This thing is a Springer Spaniel and it's got a real nose for crisps for some reason," and Carl laughed. "Well anyway, I though I saw Beth go into a cottage there. I know you will think I am nuts, but just on instinct I shouted Beth. She quickly ran up the path and went inside."

"So, then what did you do?"

"Well I had to be sure so I knocked on the door, but she wouldn't come to the door John."

"So you think Beth is alive?"

THE SORROW BEGINS

"Well I can't be sure but if she isn't then she has got a double."

They pulled up outside of Bobby Lint's house, 14 Oker Way, South Dilley Dale. His house had been a former council house. You could tell the ones that had been bought as the council had to make good the structure. So there was a midge modge of some done up, and the ones still under council ownership that hadn't been touched. Number 14 had a tidy garden and looked neat from the outside. Gammon knocked on the glass paneled door, and he could see Lint about to open it.

"Good morning Mr Lint." Gammon and Milton showed their warrant cards.

John Gammon Peak District Detective

"Could we have a few minutes of your time?"

"Yes, by all means please come in."

A golden retriever came bounding over for some fuss.

"Get down Tasha."

"Sorry about this gents, she just likes the fuss."

Lint put the dog in a back room.

"Now how can I help you?"

"Ex-army then Mr Lint?"

"Yes, did twenty years in the Para's, served everywhere; Falklands, Iraq and Belize, you name it."

"Why did you come out?"

"It was eighteen months back. I started to feel the aches and pains as you do at my age."

THE SORROW BEGINS

"What age would that be?"

"Fifty three Mr Gammon."

"Well you certainly look after yourself."

"Well I try."

"Is there a Mrs Lint?"

"No, I am afraid I was my married to my career, bit like you lads I don't doubt."

"So how long have you known the golf club crew?"

"It must be fifteen years. They are a good set of blokes and looked after me when I came out. Then I worked my way out of the army."

"In what way?"

"Well, Alec gave me a job at his warehouse business. I was there for a about two months and have worked for Freddie since then."

John Gammon Peak District Detective

"So, you work for Mr Slack?"

"Yes."

"What exactly you do you do for Mr Slack?"

"I drive for him. Freddie likes a sherbet or two, so I run him around."

"Does it pay well?"

"Yes, it's ok."

"Let's talk about Duncan Mule. You were there the night he went missing?"

"Yes, I was working for Freddie. They had all been golfing and then playing cards. eventually Duncan said he was going."

"Was he driving?"

"I don't know."

Gammon could see Lint didn't want to drop Mule in it.

THE SORROW BEGINS

"Freddie did say to me, go and check on the silly old fool. I went outside but I couldn't see him so assumed he had left."

"Was Mr Mule well liked?"

"I suppose there are people that like you and people that don't, so no different to any of us. Although I will say his wife, well now there is a different kettle of fish. They call her the Queen at the golf club, she is that far up her arse."

"So, she isn't well liked?"

"I would say not."

"Ok Mr Lint, thank you for your cooperation we will be in touch."

On the way out Milton spotted a Glock 17 pistol, having been in Rapid Response he knew his guns.

"I hope that's decommissioned Sir."

John Gammon Peak District Detective

"I can assure you it is DI Milton," and he handed Milton the pistol. Milton looked at it.

"Yes, I can see it is. Ever been fired in anger Mr Lint?"

"Yes, I killed three extremists in Afghanistan, only the second day after it was issued to me. I won the Military Medal for that. I saved three colleagues from certain death by storming the safe house."

"Ok Mr Lint we will speak again."

Gammon and Milton got back in the car.

"Seems like a nice guy and served his country well."

Gammon didn't reply to Milton.

"What are you thinking John?"

THE SORROW BEGINS

"Never judge a book by its cover Carl. I am a bit older than you so probably a bit wiser."

They arrived at Iman Oglee's flat, No 4 Old Road, Dilley Dale. Not the most salubrious of places they both thought. They climbed the short amount of steps to the flat and knocked on the door. Iman answered she was still in her dressing gown. Gammon thought he was going to have to close Milton's gaping mouth.

"Can I help you?"

They showed their warrant cards.

"Just want a few minutes of your time, if that's ok Iman?"

She hesitated but then agreed. Gammon could immediately smell the sweet smell of Marijuana. He wasn't too concerned, they

John Gammon Peak District Detective

hadn't come about that. The flat was a bit like a student's; dirty pots in the sink, a cereal bowl on the side and a pizza box with a half-eaten pizza still in the open box. Iman sat crossed legged which left little to the imagination.

"How well do you know Duncan Mule?"

"He is just a guy that comes into the golf club. I don't know him socially."

"Would you say he is well liked?"

"I don't know Mr Gammon."

"Do they tip you well?"

"Yes of course, I play up to them. They all think they have a chance, but they don't. It makes me about three hundred pounds a week in tips so I don't mind."

"How old are you Iman?"

THE SORROW BEGINS

"Twenty nine."

"Your boss at the golf club, do you get on?"

Iman hesitated.

"Yes, I suppose so."

"So, you are not close friends then?"

"No."

"Ok, well thanks for your time Iman, we will be in touch."

Iman showed them out.

"Put your tongue away Carl."

"She is gorgeous John."

"We shall see, I think she is hiding something."

"Like what?"

"Not sure yet."

They arrived at Maggie Silitoe's. She lived at Billy Morris Farm in Hittington.

John Gammon Peak District Detective

The farm wasn't exactly in Hittington, but John could remember Billy Morris when he was a kid and when he died it was always known as Billy Morris farm. It looked like she, or the previous owners, had spent a lot of money on the farm. It wasn't anything like a working farm as John could remember. Gammon knocked on the oak door and a lady answered.

"Mrs Silito?"

"No, actually Ms Silito. Who's asking?"

Gammon and Milton produced their warrant cards. Silito seemed genuinely shocked.

"What's the problem?"

THE SORROW BEGINS

"I just wondered if we could have a chat. We are looking into the disappearance of Duncan Mule."

Silito showed them into the big farmhouse kitchen with its flag floors and large Rayburn cooker. This reeked of money Milton thought.

"So, can I call you Maggie?"

"Yes, not a problem."

"So, Maggie you are the bar manager at the golf club, is that correct?"

"Yes."

"Must pay very well, if you don't mind me saying."

"It pays ok."

"This is some place you have here."

"Yes, I like it."

She wasn't playing Gammon's game.

John Gammon Peak District Detective

"Tell me what you know about Duncan Mule."

"I know he plays golf. Also I know he is a dirty old buggar, always coming out with suggestive remarks to me and my staff."

"Does that offend you?"

"Not in the slightest, he tips well Mr Gammon."

"What about his wife?"

"Who her Royal Highness, Pamela?" Gammon smiled.

"I take you are not to keen on her?"

"Spot on Mr Gammon, your powers of deduction are intact."

"So, you really have no clue where Mr Mule may have gone?"

THE SORROW BEGINS

"Not a clue, and if you don't mind I need to get ready for the Golf Club."

"Ok Ms Silito, we will be in touch."

Gammon and Milton headed back to the car.

"What are your thoughts John?"

"What about Maggie Silito?"

"Yes."

"Well let's be honest, she hasn't got that place and car by working as a bar manager at the golf club. I think we can dig a bit deeper Carl for tomorrow's meeting. Let's see what surprises we bring up."

The following day Carl was well prepared. He had stayed late that night and come in early that morning. John set off from the cottage at 8.00 am. He hadn't been feeling to good all night. As he sat in his

John Gammon Peak District Detective

Jaguar he suddenly felt a searing hot burning sensation shoot up his spine. He knew what that probably was, the bullet and shrapnel lodged near his spine. He put the heated seats on, which tended to help when he wasn't too good and he set off for Bixton. All the fields on the back road were covered in frost making a magical scene.

He wound his way round the little lanes before eventually joining the main road for the last three miles into work. John always felt how lucky he was to live in the beautiful Peak District, even if sometimes his desire to enhance is career reared its ugly head. By the time he pulled up at Bixton Police Station his back felt ok, and John being John, put it to the back of his

THE SORROW BEGINS

memory. By 9.00am everyone was in the incident room. John and Amanda went in.

"Ok everybody, there has been no sightings of Duncan Mule and because of him and his wife's connection things are hotting up. So, let's start off with DI Scooper."

"Ok, well myself and DI Lee visited Freddie Slack's home. We were greeted by his wife Sondra, not a particularly pleasant woman. She said Freddie was having a lie-in and she wasn't too pleased when we said she had to wake him. We waited in the hall way. It was a sumptuous house, down a small lane. It must have had sixteen bedrooms, it could have been a hotel. Slack said good morning and shook hand. He said what's the problem? Mule's wife had been on the phone all night to Sondra. She is a bloody drama queen. He thought that Mule had found himself a floozy and was having a good time. Both me and DI Lee felt the vibe that this man didn't give a toss for anyone. We went through his story which pretty much seemed believable, but we left both thinking there is more to come further down the line."

"We then headed for Alec Blake's home in Ackbourne. Blake's house was a lot more conservative although still about a five bedroom property on a nice estate. Mr Blake was very co-operative I took this to mean I could push him on what he thought of Freddie Slack. He clammed up on the mention of his name saying Freddie was a

THE SORROW BEGINS

good guy, not everyone's cup of tea but an all round good guy. You know when somebody is saying something they don't actually believe, and that is what myself and DI Lee thought."

"Anything else Sandra?"

"No, that's it."

"Ok, well I would like you and DI Lee to look into their bank accounts. Look for the usual stuff, anything where we can get a lead from please."

Sandra nodded.

"Ok Dave, what did you and Magic find?"

DI Smarty came to the front. Dave Smarty was in his mid fifties and had been a copper a long time so he knew how the world went round.

"Well to be honest both Thorndyke and Wilkins were very cooperative. Both guys retired early, enjoy their golf and the club house banter, but other than that didn't feel any concerns."

"Ok, well if you all look into your respective interviewees' bank accounts and if you find anything come and see me. Myself and DI Milton spoke with Lint, Oglee and Silito and we both have concerns they are hiding something. What that something is we don't know, but Carl will be looking in depth at their bank records etc like you all."

As everyone started to disperse.

"Sir."

"Yes, Sergeant Yap."

THE SORROW BEGINS

"We may have found Duncan Mule. I just took a call from a Mrs Clunson who said her son has just found a body near the football pitch. I have sent a squad over to cordon off the area and forensics are on their way."

"Brilliant Sergeant Yap."

"Are you coming Ma'am?"

"I wouldn't miss it for the world," DCI Cook replied.

Gammon and Cook headed to a recreation park in Mill Dale some seventeen miles from Bixton. On the way Amanda Cook started to question Gammon about his health.

"How are you John?"

"I have noticed you wincing now and again. It's the bullet problem isn't it?"

"Oh, I am ok."

John Gammon Peak District Detective

"John, work will be here when you are not, at least get it checked out."

"Suppose you are right."

"I am. In fact when we get back I am going to make an appointment for you."

John thought how great it was to have such a caring boss.

They arrived at Mill Dale and wandered under the tape to the white incident tent.

"What we got Wally?"

"White male, possibly sixty two, he has lacerations on his back, but at the moment that's as far as I have got."

"Could you have a positive identification by 9.00am?"

"Slave driver, but yes I guess so."

"Cheers mate, top man as usual."

THE SORROW BEGINS

"Think we best go and speak with Pamela Mule before the press boys get wind of it. This should be fun. Amanda, have you met her yet?"

"I have seen her at Police Federation meetings. What a flippin' prima donna."

Gammon and Cook arrived at Dove Dale Towers. The house, a former residence of Lord and Lady Saxwell, it is believed to be where Sir Isaac Newton often stayed while fly fishing in the river Dove. The house was magnificent with turreted walls, small windows and even a small moat that ran around the outside of the main building. A butler opened the massive old door and showed them into the drawing room, while he fetched Pamela Mule. Pictures adorned the walls of the room all depicting Duncan

John Gammon Peak District Detective

Mule and his Formula One career. Pamela Mule strode in.

"What do you have for me Gammon?" she barked.

"Good afternoon Mrs Mule. This is DCI Cook."

"Yes, yes, get on with it man, it's my afternoon of bridge with my ladies."

"We are very sorry to tell you that a body has been found at Mill Dale and we have reason to believe it is that of Mr Mule."

Pamela Mule stood transfixed. Gammon called the butler and asked him to get Pamela Mule a glass of water.

"We will need you to identify the body Mrs Mule."

THE SORROW BEGINS

Mrs Mule just nodded, she was in complete shock. Three well dressed women, clearly from the bridge set, came through. One of the women said she would take Mrs Mule to the morgue this afternoon to identify the body.

Gammon and Cook left a shaken Mrs Mule with her friends and rang Wally to say Mrs Mule would be at the morgue at 5.00pm that evening. Wally wasn't too pleased as he said it would interfere with his findings.

John left for the night and headed up to see Saron. He was still quite annoyed with her over her possible new partnership with Jamie Mixom. You can guess who was the first person John saw as he walked into the Tow'd Man.

John Gammon Peak District Detective

"Evening John boy."

John could feel the hairs on the back of his neck stand up. He didn't answer Mixom.

"Saron about?"

"Yes, she is prepping in the kitchen."

John went to go through.

"John, sorry mate, I'll shout her. I don't like to see customers wandering into the kitchen, it sets the wrong tone.

"Saron, Saron, lover boy is here."

Saron came out. John was too annoyed to speak.

"You ok John?"

He was lost for words he wanted to punch Mixom's lights out. John looked over at him. He had a tight checked shirt, with tight trousers and cowboy boots.

THE SORROW BEGINS

"Just told John about the kitchen rules Saron. I don't think he is too happy with me, are you Sherlock?"

"That's it."

John leaped the bar and grabbed Mixom's scrawny neck. Saron ran behind the bar.

"What are you doing? Get off him John."

Two holidaymakers sitting by the bar, drank up and walked out.

"You have been goading me Mixom," he said tightening his grip. Let this be a warning to you. You cross me again and I won't be responsible for my actions," and John let go.

Mixom was holding his throat and coughing.

John Gammon Peak District Detective

"John go up to my flat. What's wrong with you?"

Gammon stared at her, and knew he had to get away, so he turned and walked out of the pub leaving Saron checking on Mixom. He drove off straight away knowing Saron would have been shouting the odds. He decided to drive to the Wobbly Man. For a big pub it was quite empty with some young college lad behind the bar.

"Pint of Haymaker please son."

The lad looked at him disinterestedly. This really wasn't what John needed after the prat at the Tow'd man.

"Is Rick about?"

"Who?"

"Rick."

"Don't know."

THE SORROW BEGINS

A voice from the other end shouted. "He is on holiday John."

"Joni? Hey, would you like a drink?"

"Go on then looks like I have been stood up."

"By who?"

"Oh, only a girl from work. She wasn't sure if she could get a babysitter for the night anyway."

"So, what are you doing in Toad Holes?"

"Just fancied a change. They say a change is as good as a rest, don't they?"

"I believe so John. Why are you not at the Tow'd Man? I hear Saron has got a hunky new partner."

"Don't go there Joni."

"Bit of jealousy going on there Mr Policeman?"

John Gammon Peak District Detective

"No, the guy is such a prat, Joni. I can't understand Saron."

"Oh, I can."

"What do you mean?"

"She is giving you some of your own medicine."

"Do you think?"

"I don't think, I know," and she laughed.

"Have you seen Carl lately?"

"No since we split he has been a bit odd with me."

"Don't think he will ever get over Beth."

"Why do you ask? He is ok, isn't he?"

"Yeah fine, but he said he thought he saw Beth going into a cottage in Snowerton Lane."

THE SORROW BEGINS

"You are kidding me. Poor Beth is dead, we all know that. I mean if she wasn't why would she leave all that money for me and Carl?"

"I don't know Joni. I agree it is a bit odd but you know what the poor girl went through."

Joni sat with a small tear running down her cheek.

"Do you think it's possible she could be alive John?"

"I have been in this game a long time Joni, and anything is possible with MI5 or MI6."

"I am going to ring Carl and see what he found out. Did he go to the cottage?"

"He never said, we have had quite a hectic few days at work."

"Carl, it's Joni."

John Gammon Peak District Detective

"Oh yeah sorry, of course you have caller identification. What are you doing?"

"Just about to take Crisps for a walk. Me and John are in the Wobbly. Why don't you call for one?"

"Ok, only be a quick one mind, or Crisps will keep me up all night."

The phone went dead.

"Carl is on his way."

"Best get another round in then. What are you drinking? I know Carl will want a Stella."

"Can I have a double vodka and coke please John?"

Joni felt quite excited at the thought that she might have John to herself tonight. John had just sat down with the drinks when the door flew open and Carl arrived

THE SORROW BEGINS

being dragged by an over zealous Springer Spaniel. It smelt the crisps John had just bought for them and made a beeline for them. Joni and John were more interested in saving the drinks than the crisps.

"So sorry about this you two."

"Don't be daft, I think it's quite funny."

Crisps just looked up as she was polishing off bag number two.

"I do now see what you mean by her name though."

"She is bloody obsessed John. She will settle down in a minute, well I hope so anyway."

"So, what are you two doing down here?"

"Well I was let down by a mate from work, she couldn't get a babysitter."

John Gammon Peak District Detective

"I just popped in for a quiet pint and saw Joni and she said she was going to call you. Stella for you Carlos?"

"Thanks John."

"Joni, did John tell you I think I saw Beth yesterday?"

"He just mentioned it, but are you sure?"

"Well I can't be 100% and her colouring was different. It's Saturday tomorrow, will you come with me? Not sure I want to knock on a woman's door on my own."

"Ok what time?"

"Can we say 10.00am?"

"Yeah fine by me."

THE SORROW BEGINS

Carl finished his Stella, and got the other two a drink, and left taking Crisps back home.

John Gammon Peak District Detective

CHAPTER THREE

By 11.00pm the Wobbly man was shutting.

"Are you coming back for a night cap John?"

The old John would have jumped at the chance she said. John knew she was right but at some point he had to be true to Saron.

"Well your choice."

Sensing Joni felt a bit annoyed, he agreed. John left his car in the Wobbly Man car park and headed up the hill to Joni's cottage. It was a cold night, but crisp and fresh. As they wandered up the hill Joni put her arm through John's. He had got his hand in his coat pocket. She snuggled her head onto John.

THE SORROW BEGINS

Once inside the cottage they took of their coats and Joni poured them a brandy each. John took a sip and whether it was the beer, the longing, or just pure lust John kissed her. Within a few minutes of gentle play they were making love. Joni's toned body writhed under John's for what seemed like an age before the sexual explosion of lust came over both of them. Joni took John's hand and led him up stairs. They lay on her king size bed with its white Egyptian cotton sheets and talked.

"Are you ok John?" she asked.

"Yes, you know the sad thing Joni, is that I promised myself at our engagement party that I would no longer be unfaithful to Saron. She doesn't deserve it. The thing is, I have already broken that vow."

John Gammon Peak District Detective

"Look John, maybe she isn't the one for you?" Saron is a lovely girl and so pretty, but has she got what John Gammon needs?"

The conversation was certainly putting doubts in John's mind. They eventually fell asleep.

The following morning they were woken by a knock on the kitchen door.

"Shit John, it's ten o clock, that will be Carl."

Joni jumped out of bed went to the top of the stairs and shouted to Carl that she would only be a minute.

"Joni, he can't see me here."

"Just stay quiet, your car is at the Wobbly. I will lock the front door. Just go

THE SORROW BEGINS

through the back door and leave the key under the stone trough when you leave."

She kissed John, "Thank you for a lovely night. We must do it again sometime."

Joni hurried downstairs to Carl.

"Sorry Carl, I overslept."

"You and John must have had a good session, his car is still in the Wobbly."

"Yeah, too many. John ordered a taxi that dropped me off and took him home. He said he was going to walk back for it sometime today."

Carl seemed happy with the explanation, he was more excited that his Beth might still be alive.

Joni and Carl arrived at Snowerton Lane.

John Gammon Peak District Detective

"I did knock on the door the other day but she wouldn't come to the door, Joni. I thought if you are with me she might."

"Now you tell me."

They approached the little cottage door and Carl rang the bell. After a few minutes a man in his late seventies answered the door. He was slightly stooped with what looked like curvature of the spine.

"How can I help you?"

"Well I'm not sure, do you have a girl living here."

"No young man I don't. I have lived here fifteen years, twelve of those on my own since my dear wife passed away."

Carl was stuck for words.

"Could I ask what your name is please?"

THE SORROW BEGINS

"Why would you want to know that young man?" the man replied in a curt manner.

"I am sorry I wasn't being rude."

"It's Coburn, Harry Coburn. Now if you don't mind I am missing my cricket," and he shut the door.

"Looks like you were wrong Carl."

"I know I saw her, and she saw me. I am going to look into this a bit deeper Joni, that's why I asked what his name was."

"Well whatever gets you over Beth is fine by me mate."

Carl dropped Joni off. John had gone so she was now alone with her thoughts. What was it with John Gammon? He clicked his fingers and she came running. Thinking about it, she thought he does it to everyone.

John Gammon Peak District Detective

John had left Joni's, picked his car up and called at work with the intention of seeing Wally to get a full report on the body. Di Trimble was on the desk Ian Yap had gone to watch his beloved Derby.

"Good afternoon Sir."

"Hi Di, how are you? Has Mrs Mule been to identify the body?"

"Yes, she has Sir, sadly it was her husband."

"Ok is Wally still here?"

"Yes, he is on his own. Watch him though, he is a bit tetchy he said her coming had slowed him down."

"Thanks for the tip off Di."

Gammon headed down the corridor to Wally's office where he was busy typing

THE SORROW BEGINS

his report. It always made Gammon smile watching Wally type with one finger.

"Nearly finished if you have come to give me grief."

Gammon laughed. "Go on then, what did you find?"

"Well he definitely was involved in some kind of sexual act before he died. His back was marked which I would say was consistent to being horse whipped. He also had marks on his back as if he had been trodden on."

"Wow this all sounds interesting. Obviously none of this was shared with the deceased's wife?"

"Of course not, John. If I was a gambling man, which I am not, I would say he was into something, how do they say it 'kinky'."

John Gammon Peak District Detective

"Well I wasn't expecting that. Estimated time of death?"

"Sometime between 1.30am and 3.00pm."

"Cause of death?"

"Strangulation."

"Ok thanks Wally, that gives me something to go on."

Gammon left Wally who was still muttering on about being disturbed while he tapped away with one finger on his computer trying to finish the report.

Gammon went back to his office and did a bit of digging on Duncan Mule. He was the British glamour boy of the seventies Formula One racing scene. He won the last of his five championships for his team in nineteen seventy eight. In

THE SORROW BEGINS

seventy nine he had a bad crash in Belgium. The date was May 21st at the Circuit Zolder. Taking a left hand bend he clipped another car and his car shot into the air, somersaulting three times before coming to rest on some hay bales. It was reported that Mule was pulled out of the wreckage by two spectators before the car exploded in flames, killing one of the spectators, a Jim Spencer from Swinster. This revelation made John's mind go into overdrive. The other spectator was a Belgium man called Stefan Jordan.

Duncan Mule never drove a Formula One car again. He had made a lot of money with property portfolios in Spain, Italy, Croatia and Florida, beside his TV work. He was in the top fifty rich list for the UK.

John Gammon Peak District Detective

He married Pamela Standing who was from a very rich family in the North of England, so it was a money match made in heaven.

Gammon decided to look a bit deeper into Mule's sexual deviance and also to see if anyone could remember Jim Spencer, the man killed rescuing Mule. This made for a great excuse to call and see Kev at the Spinning Jenny. Having been there a lot of years there was very little he didn't know about the tight knit community of Swinster.

Gammon switched off his office light and said goodnight to Di Trimble on the front desk and headed for the Spinning Jenny. On the way he noticed three missed calls from Saron. He decided to call her after he had spoken with Kev. It was almost 6.50pm

THE SORROW BEGINS

when John arrived at the Spinning Jenny. Luckily Kev was behind the bar.

"Hello mate," he said but in a strange tone. "What are you drinking?"

"I'll have a pedigree please mate."

Kev was sort of twitching his head to one side. John started to laugh, "Nervous twitch mate?"

Kev carried on doing it then John realised he was telling him to look to his left. To John's horror in the corner, all cozy, were Saron and Jamie Mixom. John was fuming and wandered over. Saron was clearly drunk.

"What the hell is going on?"

"Hey John, come here give me a kiss. Where have you been?"

John Gammon Peak District Detective

"Join us lover boy," Mixom said sarcastically.

That was it. John wasn't taking anymore crap from Mixom. As Mixom stood up with a silly grin John let go, knocking him over the table and the drinks everywhere. Kev came running from behind the bar.

"What you doing lad? I can't have this. You get out of my pub," Kev said pointing at Mixom.

With his nose streaming blood and a lump appearing over his cheek Mixom stood up.

"He attacked me landlord."

"You are a bloody trouble maker and I am not having it. Now get out."

THE SORROW BEGINS

By now Doreen hearing the commotion came out from the back. She had been doing the ironing and watching her favourite programs with a glass of wine.

"What the hell happened here?" Mixom stood up looked at Gammon.

"I won't forget this jealous boy," and he staggered out holding his nose. Saron by now was crying.

"Kevin give me the car keys. I will take her home. You stay here out of the way for tonight John."

All Saron kept saying was, Why John? I wasn't doing anything wrong!"

Doreen took Saron home and settled her in bed.

John stayed talking to Kev.

John Gammon Peak District Detective

"Look mate, I am sorry, but he has had it coming since day one. I will pay for the damage."

"Don't be soft, there is no damage, just a bit of spillage on the carpet. That will soon dry."

"Give me a brandy mate, and you have one."

"I will have a quick one before Doreen gets back."

"Are you working tonight?"

"No, in fact my relief has just walked in the door."

"Tracey, how are you?"

"Good Kev."

"What's up with Saron, John? Just seen Doreen putting her in the car. She was crying and saying she hadn't done anything.

THE SORROW BEGINS

I also passed her new business partner on the top road. He was staggering a bit and looked like he had been in the ring with Mike Tyson."

"Let's just say it's a long story Tracey."

"I have bottled up and it won't get busy for another hour, then we have Swinster Guisers in tonight."

"What the hell is that?"

"Some folk from Swinster. They dress up and perform like a short play round the local pubs. Each have a collection and the money they raise goes to local village charities. I think this year it's Pritwich old age pensioners trip to York."

"How nice is that. I do love living in the Peak District Kev, with their quirky traditions."

Kev and John sat at the bar.

"Right, are you going to tell me what the outburst was for lad?"

"I will tell you in a bit, but first I don't know if you know, but Duncan Mule was found dead."

"What, the racing driver?"

"Yes mate."

"No, I didn't know."

"Did you know him?"

"Oh yes, I knew Mule."

"Me and Doreen hadn't had the pub long, he and his cronies used to come in every Thursday and every Sunday about 5.00pm. I had a couple of pretty lasses behind the bar in those days and Mule was forever trying to touch them. You know how blokes get when they have had a few. Anyway, it was one Sunday and they were

THE SORROW BEGINS

all in when Izzy's father came early. He always picked her up, nice bloke Rod. Anyway he was sitting at the end of the bar, and Izzy was collecting glasses. As she went past Mule he dropped a fiver at her feet. The poor kid just innocently bent down to give it him back. He slapped her backside and said something like, for another fiver can I ride you? Well Rod, her father, went mental he slapped him all round the pub. In fact, see that French horn with the damage on it? Mule's head hit that. So long story short, I barred him and his mates. But I do know Rod had a lot of grief from Mule. He reckoned he knew people who would sort him out."

"Did you know a Jim Spencer?"

"Yes, what a lovely lad and such a shame he died saving that prick. Do you know he had a wife and a two year old son? Duncan Mule didn't even go and see her after the accident or when she buried her husband. That was the measure of the man, John. Probably should not say this, but I don't know many people round here that will feel sorry that he is dead."

"Sounds like he was a popular guy mate."

Just then Doreen arrived back.

"Have we calmed down, Mike Tyson?"

"Sorry Doreen."

"It's not me you need to say sorry to, it's your betrothed, but I would leave that for another day if I was you."

"Let me get you a drink. What are you having?"

THE SORROW BEGINS

"I'll just a have a quick vodka and diet soda, then I am going back to my pile of ironing and my TV programs. And you, bugger lugs, don't be getting my Kevin drunk, you hear me?"

"I'm not the bad influence here Doreen, it's Kev."

"Hey, don't blame me mate."

Doreen finished her drink but did say that John could stay if he wanted.

"Bloody hell, my wife is a diamond, isn't she John?"

"She sure is mate."

The pub filled up and John was feeling quite pleased with the information he had on Duncan Mule.
The Swinster Guisers came, did their act, and left to head for the Tow'd Man.

John Gammon Peak District Detective

"Think it's bottle of brandy time, then you can tell me why you decided to lose it with Saron's business partner lad."

Kev was a wily old fox, he knew he would get the information out of John.

"Ok I will tell you. Pour the brandy mate."

"Saron had interviewed the prat I lost it with tonight, and we had a small falling out over her making him her business partner. I could tell he was trouble. Each time I have seen him he has given me sarcastic remarks, then he did it again tonight mate."

Kev looked at him as only Kev could do.

"Are you sure it's not something else? I have known you many years mate and that outburst tonight wasn't like you."

THE SORROW BEGINS

"Look Kev, I adore Saron and one minute I think I want to settle down, then the next minute I succumb to temptation, and feel dreadful that I have let her down."

"Well lad the only advice I can give you is don't follow your heart follow your head. That's how I do things."

"Ok mate, anyway enough crap, let's get drinking this bottle of brandy."

By 1.00am the pub had emptied both Kev and John were wobbly on their feet and Doreen was locking up.

"Right, favourite copper, you first," and Doreen helped him to one of the guest rooms to sleep it off. On her return Kev was flaked out snoring like a Banshee, so she woke him and took him into bed.

John Gammon Peak District Detective

Doreen had twenty four breakfasts to do the following morning so she left John and Kev as long as she could, but by 9.45am their breakfast was ready. Both of then sat in breakfast room looking like death warmed. Doreen placed the two big breakfasts in front of them.

"When will you two ever learn?"

They both looked sorry for themselves. Eventually John almost finished his breakfast Kev went back to bed. John thanked Doreen and drove back to his cottage. On entering the hallway there was the usual amount of post from credit card companies about PPI, but then a letter with a Canadian stamp on it. John was intrigued. He poured himself a strong black coffee and sat at the kitchen table with the light

THE SORROW BEGINS

streaming through highlighting the beautiful view.

'Hi John

Hope my letter finds you well. Sorry I haven't been in touch, but you understand how my job is. I am currently in Manitoba Canada. A usual dual operation between the French and the Brits.

Obviously can't say what I am doing, but I met a charming guy the other night who he said he was a friend, so thought I would let you know. He said his name was Clive Wiggledon. He said he was at school with you and your friend Steve.

I spent the night chatting with him, he had so many stories. You must be very close friends because he was adamant I let you know he is ok and doing well John.

I am not allowed to e mail while I am on ops or call anyone, and would probably be in big trouble for writing to you, but I thought what the hell. I always feel so bad not being in touch more often.

Take care John

Your loving sister Fleur

Xxx'

John immediately called Amanda Cook. He wasn't sure what to do because he could not compromise Fleur, but he didn't want Wiggledon getting away.

THE SORROW BEGINS

John arranged for Amanda to call at the cottage, and she arrived some thirty minutes later.

"Wow John, you look rough, was it that good a night?"

"Just a bit Amanda."

"So what is this about?"

"I am going to show you a letter from my sister, but you have to promise me what I tell you goes no further."

"Blimey John, it all sounds a bit John Le Carre."

"Trust me, it is."

"My sister works for MI5 and MI6 and also the French Secret Service."

"Oh, runs in the family eh?"

"She is always on covert operations, and she would normally never contact me at

John Gammon Peak District Detective

these times, but I got a letter from her today," and John handed Amanda the letter.

Amanda pulled her Dolce & Gabbana spectacles out of her glasses case and promptly read the letter.

"John, this is incredible. Are you able to contact your sister? If we just knew where in Manitoba she was."

"No, and she would probably lose her career if we tried to find out where she is. It's a long story but she is kind of a double agent. She is really working for the British Government but the French think she works for them."

"I know what we can do. We let the powers know we have had an anonymous tip off that Wiggledon is in Manitoba Canada, but we don't know where. Let's

THE SORROW BEGINS

see if shaking the tree will bring any fruit as they say."

"I'll do that right away and I suggest you go back to bed," and she laughed.

Amanda left to sort what they had discussed, and John took her advice to go back to bed. His head felt like there was a guy playing a big base drum inside it. He slept through to 7.00am Monday morning, so he showered and dressed, and went into work early.

"Good morning Sergeant Yap. How did your lads get on Saturday?"

"We beat Bolton 6-1 Sir, we were awesome."

"Oh ok."

Gammon wasn't a big football fan, and he knew Ian Yap would speak for hours on

John Gammon Peak District Detective

the subject. He headed for his office before he got chance, telling Yap to get all the staff in the incident room for 9.00am as he walked away. Gammon felt refreshed. DI Cook wasn't in today, but said she would call once she got out of her meeting. Gammon entered the incident room. DI Milton had put the picture up of Duncan Mule's body showing the lacerations on his back, the strangulation marks on his neck etc.

"Good morning everyone. Are we all here?"

"DI Scooper's daughter is sick, so she has had to take the day off today?"

"Ok, thanks Carl."

THE SORROW BEGINS

"On Saturday I came in to find John Walvin and discuss the body of Duncan Mule. So, Wally let us have the report."

Wally stood up and began.

"The victim was identified as Duncan Mule by Pamela Mule. On close inspection of the body I have deduced that the victim was strangled and dumped at the park. Sometime before he died he had been involved in a sexual encounter. We found semen on his body. He also had lacerations on his back."

Wally pointed to the picture.

"These were found to be consistent with possibly a horse whip. There were also indentations and redness where it appears somebody had maybe walked up his back in stiletto heels."

John Gammon Peak District Detective

Smarty and Lee were laughing. "Lucky beggar," Lee said.

"Ok, thanks Wally. Right, well I have been asking about and some interesting things came out. Duncan Mule had a bad accident in Belgium at Circuit Zolder. He was rescued by two spectators, but unluckily a local man, a Mr Jim Spencer from Swinster, was fatally wounded by the car exploding. Spencer had a son and was married. Could his son hold a grudge? I intend to visit Jim Spencer's wife, with DI Smarty, to delve a bit deeper. I would like DI Lee and Sergeant Magic to question a gentleman called Rod Goff. Many years ago he had an altercation with Mule in the Spinning Jenny, with regard to inappropriate behaviour towards his then

THE SORROW BEGINS

young daughter. Ok anybody got anything else?"

Nobody said anything.

"Ok, let's see what we can find." Gammon wanted to say about Wigbledon to the team but knew he couldn't.

Milton had found the address of Mrs Spencer so they drove to Swinster. The Spencer house hung to the side of a hillside overlooking the valley, the view was spectacular. The white house was neat and tidy but for a few children's toys. A woman in her late sixties answered the door.

"Can I help you?"

Gammon flashed his warrant card.

"Oh dear, what is this about? It's not Robinson, is it?"

"Robinson, madam?"

"Yes, my son Robinson Spencer."

John Gammon Peak District Detective

"Sorry, no. I just wanted to ask you a few questions."

"Do come in. Would you like a drink?"

"That's very good of you Mrs Spencer. I'll have a tea, white, no sugar."

"Same for me," Milton replied. Mrs Spencer came back with their teas and two pieces of lemon drizzle cake.

"Very kind of you Mrs Spencer."

"Please call me Dorothy."

"Ok thank you Dorothy."

"Oh, and I'm not Spencer anymore, my married name is Hampton."

"Well, Hampton it is Dorothy. A couple of days ago a Mr Duncan Mule was found dead."

Dorothy went deadly quiet.

THE SORROW BEGINS

"You think it's Robinson, don't you Mr Gammon?"

"Why do you say that?"

"Well everybody knows what happened a few years back, but he has grown up. He is now married with two kiddies of his own hence the toys everywhere. His wife just picked them up so I haven't had chance to tidy up."

"What was the incident?"

"Robinson was only two when his dad died, and it was tough up bringing him up on my own. He often had to have clothes from the charity shop in Micklock to go to school in, and he was teased relentlessly by the kids. Children can be cruel and they said his dad had been kicked by a Mule. I think this festered inside him. When he was eighteen I met a kind caring man, Sam

Hampton, but Robinson by now was quite wayward. Sam tried to get him back on the right track but the harder he tried the more Robinson went the other way. One night I don't know if he had been drinking or had taken something, but he took four cans of fuel that Sam kept for the mower. He allegedly went to Mule's house and decided to set fire to the garage hoping it would spread. Luckily or unluckily depending on your point of view Duncan Mule was away with business, but Pamela Mule arrived back from playing Bridge, and she caught him red handed. Robinson panicked and hit Pamela knocking her to the ground. Then she said he kicked her several times round the head. Somebody had called the fire brigade and two police cars arrived as well.

THE SORROW BEGINS

Robinson was arrested. We could not afford a lawyer worth his salt and they had the best. The judge sent him down for eleven years. He was let out after eight years on good behaviour. He blamed Mule and still does to this day, for the road his life took him on. Mule never thanked the family or tried to help us financially in any way. We could not claim any life insurance because they said he had gone into a non-spectator area. It was all such a mess Mr Gammon, but my boy is now settled with a lovely girl and two lovely children. They rent a little cottage in Cowdale and Robinson works as a delivery driver for Van Man. I am very proud of the way he has turned his life round Mr Gammon."

John Gammon Peak District Detective

"Ok Dorothy, I am pleased for you, but I could do with a chat with Robinson. Could you write down his address please?"

Dorothy grabbed a page from a notebook and wrote Nut Kiss Cottage, Cowdale and the postcode.

"Thank you very much for your time Dorothy."

Gammon and Milton left with Dorothy looking anxious. Gammon could sense she thought Robinson was capable of murder because of his hatred of Mule.

THE SORROW BEGINS

CHAPTER FOUR

"What do you think John?"

"It's a bit concerning Carl, I must say."

Carl drove them to Cowdale village with its little duck pond, paper shop come general store, and a couple of pubs.

"Always thought I could live here John, it always seems like time stands still in Cowdale."

"Let's hope time has moved on for Robinson, hey Carl?"

"Guess so John."

Nut Kiss Cottage was a delightful small cottage, possibly only two bedrooms with a small handkerchief size front garden. Gammon knocked on the door and Robinson Spencer came to the door. Spencer was about six foot tall with a tattoo

John Gammon Peak District Detective

sleeve on his left arm depicting Marilyn Monroe, and what looked like Barry Sheen and his number seven motorbike.

"Sorry mate, if you are selling something I'm off to work in a minute."

Gammon and Milton flashed their warrant cards.

"Oh, the filth never leave an ex-con alone, do you boys?"

"It's just a few questions Mr Spencer."

"Come in then."

Spencer showed them into the kitchen. The first thing Gammon thought was how tidy the house looked.

"Ok fire away, what's the problem?"

THE SORROW BEGINS

"Well you may or may not be aware Mr Spencer, but Duncan Mule was found dead a couple of days ago."

Robinson Spencer reeled back and laughed, "So the twat has finally got what was coming to him."

"Not a fan then Mr Spencer?" Milton asked.

"What a stupid question, have you not read my file?"

DI Milton did feel a bit stupid asking the question.

"So where were you between the hours of 1.00am and 4.00am two nights ago, Mr Spencer?"

"Tucked up in bed with my wife Lou Lou."

"Will Mrs Spencer corroborate your alibi?"

"She better Inspector," and he laughed.

"Ok, for now that's all we need, but we may need to question you further Mr Spencer."

"Fine by me gents," and he showed them out.

"What do you think Carl?"

"Not sure John, but I do get the impression he was confident his wife would give him an alibi."

"Ok, let's go and see Rod Goff."

Milton drove to Swinster and a small cul-de sac on the edge of the village.

"Which one is it Carl?"

"Number seven Bircher View. Number seven, it's there, John."

THE SORROW BEGINS

Goff had a semi-detached bungalow. Gammon rang the door bell which played flower of Scotland as its ring tone. A tall man in his early sixties answered the door.

"Rod Goff?" Gammon asked as he showed his warrant card.

"Yes why?"

"DI Gammon and DI Milton Bixton police."

"How can I help you?"

"It's just a few questions Mr Goff, may we come in?"

Goff showed them into the small living room where a disabled woman was sitting in a wheelchair.

"This is my wife Adele, Mr Gammon. These policemen want to have a chat about something."

John Gammon Peak District Detective

"Ok Mr Goff, I'll get straight to the point. A couple of days ago a Mr Duncan Mule was found dead due to strangulation. We are treating this as a murder investigation."

"So, what has that got to do with me?"

"Well hopefully nothing, but some years ago I believe you had a run-in with Duncan Mule in The Spinning Jenny pub, is that correct?"

"Yes Mr Gammon, he tried to touch our young daughter up, and I did what any respectable, loving father would have done."

"Whilst I can't condone what you did, I do have sympathy Mr Goff. Could you tell me where you were two nights ago between the hours of 1.00am and 4 .00am?"

THE SORROW BEGINS

"Yes, I was in Bixton hospital with my wife. She had just had some more surgery, we were there all week only came home an hour ago."

"Could anybody vouch for you?"

"Definitely Mr Gammon."

"Ok Mr Goff, sorry to have troubled you," and Gammon and Milton left.

"There's no mileage in Rod Goff Carl, I think we can forget him.
Let's get back to the station and see if the others have found anything."

It was almost 4.00pm when Gammon was alerted to a disturbance at Bixton Golf Club. The caller had said an altercation was happening between Roger Thorndyke, Bobby Lint and a local builder, Phil Sterndale. Gammon decided to attend since two of the deceased Duncan Mule's friends were involved.

"Come on Sergeant Magic, let's find out what's going on."

Gammon arrived, parking round the back not wanting to upset the officious parking guy from last time. Once inside the club house there had clearly been a problem. One or two tables were still on the side and Roger Thorndyke was being comforted by Iman. He had a split lip and facial bruising.

"Now gentlemen, what have we here?"
"Nothing, just Iman being over zealous phoning you."
"How did you get your injuries?"

THE SORROW BEGINS

"It's nothing DI Gammon, I don't wish to press charges."

"What about all this damage and where is Mr Sterndale?"

"He left."

"Why did you fall out?"

Bobby Lint spoke up. "I had nothing to do with all this Mr Gammon."

"So, you are telling me this was between Mr Thorndyke and Mr Sterndale."

"Yes."

Thorndyke glanced over giving Lint a distinctly frosty look.

"So, who is paying for the damage?"

"I have told Iman to let me know how much it is and to charge it to my account."

"I deduce from that Mr Thorndyke, that you feel you were in the wrong."

John Gammon Peak District Detective

"Absolutely not, he came in here wanting trouble."

"Are you sure you don't want to take this further?"

"No thank you, Mr Gammon."

Iman was provocatively dressed and Gammon though Thorndyke was liking the attention anyway.

"Ok Sergeant Magic, let's leave." On the way out Gammon told Magic to phone the station and get them to get Phil Sterndale in for a chat at 9.00am.

Magic dropped Gammon off at the station and he headed to the Tow'd Man to see Saron. He decided to go the back way to avoid Jamie Mixom, he really didn't need the hassle. Saron was busy in the kitchen.

THE SORROW BEGINS

"Hi you ok?"

"Yes, fine thank you," she replied. You could cut the atmosphere with a knife.

"Are you still annoyed with me?"

"John, I can't believe you could be so bloody jealous, he is going to be my business partner. I don't tell you how to sort things in your job. This is my pub and I will choose whoever I want to be my partner."

Saron could be very strong willed when she wanted to be. The problem with their relationship would always be that John was also strong minded to the point of stubborn, and he wasn't giving in.

"I'm going Saron. You know where I am when you want to talk."

She turned back to cooking the steak on the griddle and John left feeling annoyed. Luckily he didn't see Mixom.

John Gammon Peak District Detective

He decided to go straight home as he was sure he wasn't good company at the minute. Roger Glazeback and his son had just finished milking.

"Hi John, not very often we see you back this early."

"Hi Roger, yeah, thought I would have an early night. How are you two?"

"Good mate thanks, can't say I am looking forward to the winter months mucking all these cows out."

"You will survive mate, you are like dad was, you love it really."

Roger and his son left and John went inside. He poured himself a large Jameson and sat with his thoughts. The situation with

THE SORROW BEGINS

Saron wasn't good, he personally could not seem to not give into temptation. His sister wasn't aware that Clive Wiggledon was a fugitive and he couldn't contact her in case it blew her cover. The Duncan Mule case didn't appear to have any leads, so all in all things were not working out. The problem with John Gammon was that if things didn't fall into place then the Jameson bottle took over. By 10.30pm he had almost finished the bottle and had nothing to eat. John staggered upstairs and fell fast asleep with the alarm waking him at 7.15am.

John headed for the shower feeling like death warmed up. He decided to dress and call at Beryl's Butties for a full English breakfast that usually straightened him out. Beryl's place was quite full with local builders, plumbers etc so John stood out a

John Gammon Peak District Detective

bit in his Paul Smith suit and highly polished shoes.

Once he had demolished the breakfast he almost immediately felt better. He paid for it and left, arriving at 8.45am at Bixton.

"Morning Sir."

"Good morning Sergeant Yap." Everything ok from last night?

"Yes, Di said it was quiet Sir. A Phil Sterndale is in interview room one for you."

"Oh, ok Ian I best go straight in then."

John entered the room. Phil Sterndale was a big chap. He had a checked work shirt and a pair work trousers on. Gammon noticed he was biting his nails as if a bit nervous.

THE SORROW BEGINS

"Good morning Mr Sterndale, DI Gammon."

"Do I need a solicitor?"

"No, you don't Mr Sterndale, this is just an informal chat, if that's ok?"

"Yeah fine by me."

"Going back to yesterday's altercation at the golf club, what was that all about?"

"Those robbing bastards."

"I'm sorry, who Mr Sterndale?"

"Mule, Slack, Thorndyke that lot."

"I'm sorry, I don't understand."

"Well let me explain. My father and mother owned a farm in Lingcliffe. We moved there ten years back. Unknown to dad at the time the farm had valuable land surrounding it. When the government relaxed building regulations a few years ago that bloody big-headed lot saw an

John Gammon Peak District Detective

opportunity. For two years Mule and his mate did everything to drive my father out. With their connections dad struggled to get help on the farm, or to sell his cows and lambs. When they had almost driven him broke they offered him two hundred and eighty thousand for the farm house buildings and one hundred and ten acres. By then dad was under the doctor for depression. Mum had died, which to this day I am sure it was the stress that brought on her illness. Dad never told me, I just assumed farming was going through a bad patch. Anyway, he sold it to their consortium, Mule Slater Associates, that set of bastards. Two days after the sale dad took his own life."

THE SORROW BEGINS

"I can see where that may cause some angst against them, but what happened yesterday?"

"I received a letter from the consortium stating that a field that dad had let me use for growing veg, and also a field I kept a few sheep on was to be no longer available for my use. It was needed for the housing estate and the road was going through the two fields. After all they had done to my family that was the last straw."

"Could I ask you, was this before Duncan Mule was found strangled?"

Phil went quiet.

"Yes, it was a day before, but I didn't have anything to do with that. But I would buy a drink for whoever did Mr Gammon."

John Gammon Peak District Detective

"So, going back to yesterday what made you go and have the altercation with Mr Thorndyke?"

"I was passing the golf club and I saw Thorndyke going in. The red mist came down so I went in and he told me to 'run along little man', so I hit him."

"Why would you think he wouldn't want to press charges Mr Sterndale?"

"Because they are all bloody bent, that's why, and they don't want it highlighting."

"Ok Mr Sterndale, but in light of what you have told me I may need to speak with you again at some point."

"I've nothing to hide Mr Gammon, unlike that thieving lot."

THE SORROW BEGINS

Phil Sterndale left the station and Gammon called a meeting in the incident room.

"Right everybody, this is what we have so far in the Duncan Mule murder. We have three suspects so far all with a reason to hate Mule. Number one Robinson Spencer; massive grudge after his father was killed rescuing Mule from a burning car. Number Two Rod Goff; had altercation after Mule came on to his daughter some years back. Personally I think we can discount him but you never know in this job. Number three Phil Sterndale; local builder, his parents were supposedly forced out of their farm so Mule and his consortium could have the land for housing. The farm was sold cheap to them and Sterndale's father committed suicide a couple of days after the farm was sold. He subsequently has been told that the two fields his father let him use for veg growing and a sheep field are no longer available to him. In a fit of anger he confronted Roger Thorndyke at the golf club yesterday. He blacked his eye cut his lip etc., but no charges were brought, bit strange that I think."

"Have we got anything else?"

"Yes, DI Smarty."

"I think so Sir. I have been looking up Maggie Silito to see if she has a criminal record. Silito came to the UK from Latvia in 2007. Her name then was Maggie Silkins, when she arrived here she changed her name by deed poll to Silito. In Latvia

THE SORROW BEGINS

she ran a prostitution racket, so I took the chance and I have watched her flat for two nights. I have seen numerous girls go in for what appears to be a two hour shift. Men go in but they all park about a quarter of a mile away and walk to the flat. I think we should raid her."

"Great work Dave, but I would like to keep this low key just at the minute. That could explain the whipping marks on Duncan Mule and maybe the strangulation."

Sergeant Yap interrupted the meeting.

"Sorry Sir but I thought it might be of interest, I have a Gayle Thorndyke in reception. She said her husband didn't come home last night."

"Put her in interview room one please Sergeant."

John Gammon Peak District Detective

"Ok everybody let's do some digging on bank accounts, of previous employments, and connections to Mule that might be dodgy."

"DI Smarty, you come with me please."

Gammon and Smarty headed for interview room one.

"Mrs Thorndyke? DI Gammon and DI Smarty."

Gayle Thorndyke looked about thirty five with long blonde hair and a decent figure. She was clearly a lot younger than Roger Thorndyke who was in his early sixties Gammon thought. He dyed his moustache jet black, which Gammon thought was odd when he met him.

"How can we help you Mrs Thorndyke?"

THE SORROW BEGINS

"Please call me Gayle."

"Ok Gayle."

"Well it's my husband, you see he went golfing yesterday with his mates as normal but he never returned. He sometimes is late. It's even been 2.00am in the past, but he is always home by the time I go to work."

"Where do you work Gayle?"

"I work in Bixton at Sutton and Carmichael the solicitors. I am a clerk and I have worked there almost ten years. Roger hates it that I work and he retired when he was fifty one. I am a lot younger than him and he employs a cleaner, gardener, and somebody to wash and iron, so there is nothing for me to do. He is out with his friends seven days a week and I am not sitting in that great big house on my own, so I work."

John Gammon Peak District Detective

Gammon was already sensing things were not good between Gayle and Roger Thorndyke.

"So, getting back to Roger, has he ever not come home?"

"Once he did, but he phoned me to say he had gone with the lads from the golf club to Amsterdam for a few days."

"Well look Gayle, I will instruct everyone to keep an eye out for him, but he is an adult and is free to do as he pleases."

"I know Mr Gammon but after what happened to Duncan Mule I thought it best I report him missing."

"Yes, not a problem Gayle we will be in touch."

THE SORROW BEGINS

"Gammon decided another trip to the golf club was in order.

"Come on Smarty, let's see what falls out when we shake the tree."

They arrived at Bixton Golf Club and duly parked round the back. The 'jobs worthy' guy was sweeping leaves up.

"You here again, you should join," and he smiled showing that he only had one front tooth.

Gammon just smiled and went up the stairs to the club house with Smarty. There was nobody in the club house, but a petite, blonde haired girl stocking the coolers with bottles.

"Oh hello," she said in a foreign accent.

"What can I get for you?"

Gammon showed his warrant card along with Smarty.

John Gammon Peak District Detective

"Do you know Roger Thorndyke?"

The girl hesitated at first.

"Yes, I know Roger."

"Do you know him well?"

The girl cleared her throat.

"Yes, I live in his flat."

"In his flat?"

"Yes, on Market Street."

"Are you having an affair with Roger Thorndyke?"

"Sort of, he comes and visits me, and he got me the job here. He is a nice man Mr Gammon."

"Did Roger Thorndyke stay at your flat last night?"

"Yes, he said he had a business meeting in London so he stayed over and caught the train."

THE SORROW BEGINS

"Are you lovers?"

"I sleep with Roger but he isn't my boyfriend. I have boyfriend in Latvia Mr Gammon."

"So basically Mr Thorndyke calls now and again but pays the bills?"

She nodded.

"So what time did he leave your flat?"

"His alarm went off at 6.00am but I fell back to sleep."

"Did he say who he was meeting in London?"

"No, he just said he had a meeting but would probably see me tonight because I am on the bar until closing."

"Thank you, Miss?"

"Petra Silvu."

"Ok thanks Miss Silvu."

John Gammon Peak District Detective

"Bloody hell, John," Smarty said as they left the club house. "She was gorgeous. How did that old goat cop for that?"

"Money talks Dave. What we have to decide is do we drop Roger the Dodger in it with his wife?"

"Well I would John, why should he have all the luck?" and DI Smarty laughed.

"I think we best let sleeping dogs lie for now."

He had no sooner said the words when Sergeant Yap rang to say a Mrs Thorndyke had rung to apologise for wasting time, but her husband had contacted her. He forgot to mention he had to go to London to a meeting.

"Ok thanks Sergeant Yap."

THE SORROW BEGINS

John dropped DI Smarty off at the station and decided to call for a quick drink and a take-away meal that Doreen would do for him. He pulled into the car-park and noticed DI Milton's car was on the car-park. He thought that Carl must be having a few beers knowing he had booked the rest of the week off.

"Evening Kev."

"Hi lad, glad you have come. Got young Milton over there feeling right sorry for himself. What are you drinking?"

"Pedigree mate please."

"You sort him out and I will bring it over John."

"Thanks Kev.

"Hi Carl, you ok?"

John Gammon Peak District Detective

Carl's voice was a bit slurred.

"I saw her John, I know I did."

"Who Carl?"

"Beth of course, I took time of work to do some digging. Me and Joni went to the cottage where I saw her go around the back."

"So, was she there then?"

"No, an old guy answered, said his name was Harry Coburn, and he had lived there for fifteen years, twelve on his own since his wife died."

"So, you got it wrong Carl."

"That's just it John, I didn't. I looked up the man's name on the electoral register. That name wasn't registered, in fact there had been no name registered for ten years. So I then checked with the local estate

THE SORROW BEGINS

agents in Micklock. They said funnily enough a Mr Barratt had rented the cottage three months ago on a long term lease, but had decided he was moving on a couple of days ago. He paid in full, and there was an envelope with the keys in it pushed through the door."

"So, what are you saying Carl? You saw Beth and she possibly saw you. Knowing her cover was blown whoever is protecting her put some old guy into the cottage for you to find?"

"Yes John."

"Carl it's all a bit far-fetched, isn't it mate?"

"I know how it sounds, and until Beth told me everything I would never have believed the things that go on with MI6, but it does happen John. I have gone over and

John Gammon Peak District Detective

over what happened that fateful night. Did I kill her with a stray bullet? I don't think so, it was one of those nutters. She always said to me that she had to keep running John."

"Look mate, my advice for what it's worth, I would leave her be. If she is alive and it was set up in some way that the funeral and everything was an elaborate hoax they did it for a reason.
Just be thankful that she may have survived. Keep it yourself, otherwise if she is alive that could put her life back in jeopardy mate."

All the time John was comforting Carl he knew that Fleur would know, if he could ever get the chance to see her.

"Right, come on mate, get to the bar. Let's have a beer."

THE SORROW BEGINS

"Thanks John I really appreciate your wisdom."

"Not sure its wisdom mate, more likely just good advice."

"Two pints of Pedigree and three large brandies Kev please."

"Did you say three large brandies John?"

"Yeah, one for me, one for Carl and one for you."

"Bloody hell, if Doreen catches me she will have my guts for garters."

"What time are you on until?"

"Only another three minutes, got a new barmaid starting, very pleasing on the eyes mate."

"Who's that?"

"You won't know her. She has just come up from London, a Latvian girl, she is

John Gammon Peak District Detective

doing three days a week. Speak of the devil this is Anouska Sutra."

"Anouska meet a couple of the locals. This Detective Inspector Carl Milton he lives in Toad Holes, and this is the famous Detective Inspector John Gammon."

"Very pleased to meet you. So you are famous, yes?"

"Take no notice of Gobby Kev, he is only pulling your leg."

"He is Gobby and he pulls my leg?"

"Sorry Anouska, just Derbyshire sayings, you will get used to them."

Milton could not take his eyes off Anouska. She was a tall girl, maybe early thirties with long blonde hair. She wore small denim hot pants, a white blouse with a dark coloured bra and numerous

THE SORROW BEGINS

necklaces dangling between her ample cleavage. Anouska went out the back to get some bottles.

"That's cheered you up lad, you can put your tongue away."

"Yes, she is nice Kev. What nights is she working?"

"She is doing six nights, won't be on Sundays, well not at the moment Carl."

"Looks like I am going to be a regular."

"Who set her on Kev, you or Doreen?"

"I did John, Doreen doesn't know yet. She has been up at her sister's for three days in Yorkshire."

"There may be trouble ahead," and John laughed.

With no Doreen to put Kev to bed after a night drinking brandy with John, the task fell to Shelley Etches.

John Gammon Peak District Detective

"Give me a hand Jack, he is done for."

"Tha in a real state old lad, damn good job Doreen isn't here. Who's locking up?"

"I'll do it Jack."

"What about sleeping beauty in the corner then mate?"

"Think I will just throw a blanket over him for tonight."

"Are you sleeping here?"

"I best. Doreen lets me stay in room one."

"Ok, well if you are ok lad me and Shelley are off home."

"Ok mate drive carefully."

"Do you drive Anouska?"

"No, I have no car?"

"Where are you staying?"

THE SORROW BEGINS

"Mr Kevin said I would get accommodation, but he didn't say where in the pub."

"Tell you what, you use room one. I'll grab a blanket and keep Carl company."

"You are kind man, Mr famous John Gammon," and she smiled.

The following morning John woke Carl.

"Come on mate time to go home."

"I should have known better than to drink with you and Kev, my mouth feels like the bottom of a budgie cage."

Just then Anouska came through with coffee and toast. She had her high heels on and just a long man's shirt, which John recognized to be his.

John Gammon Peak District Detective

"Hope you don't mind. I don't have pajamas yet and I found this in the wardrobe of room one."

She looked stunning.

"Yes, I think I left it last time I stayed."

"Oh, I am sorry, shall I take it off?"

As she said it she was pulling the shirt over her head John stopped her.

"No, no, you are fine Anouska, I don't need it."

"I will wash it and iron it for you Mr Gammon."

"Please, it's John and you don't have to do that, keep it."

"You are so kind John," and she leaned forward with the shirt gaping. Carl almost dropped his coffee when she pecked John on the cheek.

THE SORROW BEGINS

"How are you feeling this morning, Mr Milton?"

"No, please Carl is my name."

She giggled, "Ok Carl."

"I feel quite poorly."

"What time do you both work?"

"Well I am going in a minute, but Carl is on holiday all week."

"You take and show me round, Carl?" Anouska asked.

Carl felt instantly better, he was beaming.

"I would love to Anouska."

"I have to be back at 6.00pm because I meet Doreen."

Good luck with that John thought as he left Carl and Anouska, and headed home for a shower and a change of clothes.

John Gammon Peak District Detective

John pulled up outside his cottage. He could see the kitchen light on. It wasn't Phyllis his cleaner's day and he could not remember leaving a light on. John opened the front door. To his surprise two massive guys were sitting at his kitchen table.

"Hey, who are you?"

"Come in Mr Gammon. I am Nick Lane, and this is my colleague Frank Bonn."

"What do you want?"

"We need to talk."

"What about?"

"Well we have a problem, Mr Gammon."

"Oh yeah, what's that?"

THE SORROW BEGINS

"An associate of yours needs to return to Derby."

"Associate of mine?"

"We work for the British Government on sensitive matters."

"And?"

"Well, Mr Brian Lund."

"What about him? He is no more, and the world is a better place without him."

"It's not quite that simple. Mr Lund is a major informant for the British Government."

"What do you mean? He is bloody dead."

"Mm, not quite Mr Gammon."

This was the bit when Gammon could not say he had seen him dead, or they would know he had been at the scene. But he remembered what Fleur had said that she

John Gammon Peak District Detective

beat him to it, and surely she would not lie to him on something as important.

"We need to bring Mr Lund back to Derby. There has been a massive influx of Romanian drug cartels across the country, and Derby is a main highway for the drug trade."

"So, you are telling me that bastard is still alive?"

"Oh, very much so. He has been living in Portugal. Mr Lund has agreed to come back but only on the promise that you, Mr Gammon, leave him alone."

"I don't bloody believe this, it's like something from the movies. What if I don't leave him alone, then what?"

"All I am willing to say is for your own health, and safety of your friends you would

THE SORROW BEGINS

be well advised. The bigger picture is way more important than a country cop. Do we make ourselves clear?"

Gammon was fuming with himself, with these two idiots, with Fleur for lying to him, but most of all for being forced into allowing Lund back on the streets with all his nasty ways.

"I hope the situation is crystal clear Mr Gammon, and that we won't have to bother you again. Good day, Mr Gammon," and they calmly walked out of John's cottage.

John Gammon Peak District Detective

CHAPTER FIVE

John sat at his kitchen table feeling crest fallen. Why would Fleur of all people lie to him? So, Lund does all he did and he is allowed to come back onto the streets of Derby, and just start up again like nothing has happened. John had lost his whole family because of Lund. When he thought he was dead it was the happiest day of his life and now it had been snatched away.

It was 9.00am when his phone rang, he was now running late.

"John, where are you?" DCI Cook said sounding quite abrupt.

"Oh, I'm sorry Amanda, something came up."

THE SORROW BEGINS

"Well something came up here. We have another murder. Roger Thorndyke was found by his wife in his greenhouse, he had been strangled to death."

"I am on my way over."

"Wally is already there."

"Ok Amanda see you there, sorry about this."

Amanda ended the call so John quickly changed and headed for Riverside Mill, Dilley Dale, the grand home of Thorndyke. Gammon arrived at the Victorian mansion and headed round the back. The gardens were manicured, in fact the whole place looked immaculate.

"Morning John"

"Morning Ma'am, what have we got?"

"Well Mrs Thorndyke had gone to water the tomato plants and she found Mr

John Gammon Peak District Detective

Thorndyke slumped in a chair. She called for an ambulance and the paramedics called us when they saw the neck wounds. They couldn't do anything, he was already dead."

"Ok, I will just have a chat with Gayle Thorndyke."

Gammon walked up the lawn and tapped on the patio doors. He could see Gayle on the phone. She gestured to come in. Gayle finished her phone conversation. Gammon could see that her husband's death had shaken her, but not in a I have lost the love of my life way, he thought.

"Sorry to have to ask you these questions Gayle, but can you run through exactly what happened?"

"Well as I told you, Roger had called to say he had forgot he wouldn't be back

THE SORROW BEGINS

because he had a meeting. He said not to forget to water the tomatoes because the gardener was on a day's holiday. I got up this morning and before I was going to work I popped down to the greenhouse. As you can see, it's a very big greenhouse and we always keep the door shut because of losing heat. The first thing I noticed was the door was wide open. Anyway, I assumed the wind must have blown it open. I got the watering can and started watering. Right at the back is a small area where the potting takes place. I could see a pair of legs and beige coloured shoes. These shoes were Roger's favourites so I called out, 'Roger are you there?' Nobody answered so I walked up to the back of the greenhouse. I reeled back. Roger was slumped on the old wooden chair that Stan the gardener uses.

John Gammon Peak District Detective

At first I thought he was asleep so I shook him, but then I realised he wasn't breathing. I called 999 and the paramedics arrived very quickly, I might add. They said they couldn't do anything for him and they called the police. Nobody has told me anything yet Mr Gammon."

"Ok, well sit down, Gayle. I am afraid it looks like Roger was strangled. Until I have a full report I won't know if it was murder or not, or even if he died here, or his body was brought here. I need to ask you some in depth questions if I may?"

"Yes Mr Gammon, go ahead."

"Were you and Mr Thorndyke a couple in the full sense?"

"If you mean did I sleep with Roger, then no we hadn't been a proper couple for

THE SORROW BEGINS

over eight years. I lost a baby at twenty weeks. Roger blamed me because I had been on a girls' skiing break, and I fell over and miscarried the baby. He never forgave me, and it's been down-hill since then."

"Did you know Roger had a flat in Market Street?"

"Yes, I knew all about his infidelities Mr Gammon, but he never knew that I knew. It was best that way."

"Were you seeing anybody?"

Gayle hesitated, "Yes there is somebody special in my life."

"May I ask who?"

"I would prefer not to say Mr Gammon."

"Gayle, I really don't want to pry. Your private life is your own business, but I have to cover every angle. There is a fair chance

John Gammon Peak District Detective

your husband was murdered, and I need to ensure no stone is left unturned."

Gayle thought for a few seconds.

"Bobby Lint she blurted out. I am seeing Bobby Lint."

"Your husband's friend?"

"Well it may seem like that to everyone on the outside."

"What do you mean?"

"They were golfing friends, but Roger was the one that wouldn't let Bobby in on the land deal."

"Is this the deal where the consortium bought a farmhouse and land, and are building executive houses on?"

"Yes, I believe so. To be honest I tried to keep out of his business affairs. I keep out of his way altogether since we lost the

THE SORROW BEGINS

baby. I am sure he would have divorced me had it not been for the fact I would have got possibly half of everything."

"Did he have any enemies?"

"Does a bee make honey Mr Gammon? Nobody liked him, not even the consortium that he played golf with."

"Ok Gayle, I may have to question you again but for now that will do. Thank you for your honesty and if there is anything you have forgotten to tell me, here is my card. Call me at any time, day or night." Gammon left Gayle. By now DCI Cook and the forensic team had left the site. John made his way back to the station. On the way he took a call from Saron.

"John, I'm sorry I have been such a bitch. You were right about Mixom. I have

John Gammon Peak District Detective

told him to leave and cancelled the partnership."

"I was only looking out for you Saron."

"I know that now. I have tonight off, let's go out."

"Ok, I'll pick you up at 7.30pm. I'm going to take you somewhere nice."

"Where John?"

"You'll see."

"Don't be a tease Gammon."

"See you at 7.30pm babe," and John cancelled the call.

He felt a bit better that was sorted. Now there was just the case of two dead bodies and Clive Wiggledon to sort now.

John grabbed a coffee and went to his office. His hatred for all things that meant

THE SORROW BEGINS

he was sitting at his desk certainly showed. He must have had over fifty correspondences to open and sort. The second letter was from Fleur it simply said 'will be in touch at the weekend Fleur.' Gammon thought his day could not get much better. By the time he had waded through his paperwork it was 5.30pm. Everyone had gone so Gammon told Sergeant Yap to arrange for Bobby Lint to come in for informal questioning the following day.

"What time Sir?"

"Say 10.00am. Thanks Ian," and Gammon left. He nipped home, showered and put his Paul Smith dark blue jeans on, with a grey shirt and a blue dress coat. He had to be smart when he was taking the lovely Saron out for the night.

John Gammon Peak District Detective

John arrived at the Tow'd Man. Tracey Rodgers was working for Saron, so she smiled at John in a knowing manner.

"Come on Saron."
"Where are we going?"
"You will see."

John headed for the Christmas lights at Castlegram, a town famous for its jewelry made from a local stone called Blue John. Castlegram Christmas lights started with a few shops putting out a Christmas tree and lights some twenty years previously. Now it was massive. They parked just outside the village and walked in. Castlegram had about three inches of snow so it looked really Christmassy.

THE SORROW BEGINS

"John this is beautiful."

They wandered the little cobble streets and although there was still five weeks to Christmas brass bands were playing Carols. Saron and John passed a jewelers near the village centre, and a wedding ring took Saron's eye.

"Oh John, look at that."

"Do you like it?"

"Yes, it's lovely."

"Well let's go inside and see."

They asked the young girl to show them the ring on tray fifty three.

"Oh John," Saron became emotional. It was a platinum ring with a small band of Blue John in it.

"Do you want it?"

"I would love it, but when will we get married?"

John Gammon Peak District Detective

"Up to you."

"Shall we make it extra special and get married Christmas Day?"

"If that's what you want."

Saron flung her arms round John.

"I do love you Mr Gammon."

"I love you too," he said.

The ring was a whopping three thousand eight hundred pounds, but John didn't have a second thought. He knew she was right of him. It was he who had to ensure this worked.

They left the shop as the snowflakes came down settling on the Christmas tree that stood outside every shop, pub and restaurant.

THE SORROW BEGINS

"Oh John, this is so perfect. You make me so happy."

John smiled he also felt good inside.

"Come on, let's celebrate."

The Kings Head just of the main street of the village was built in 1605. It was now a Gastro pub but still retained its charm. Outside were Carol singers. They were like a pair of love struck teenagers as they went inside. Both rooms had big roaring log fires and Saron managed to get a table by the fire as a couple were leaving.

"What are we drinking and eating?"

"Well I would like a Proseco, and I think I'll have the Castlegram Cobbler with Lyonnais potatoes and creamed cabbage please John."

John ordered a pint of Little John bitter and a trio of local sausages on a bed of

John Gammon Peak District Detective

cranberry mash with onion gravy and red cabbage.

John sat back down.

"Who will marry us Christmas day?"

"The Trissington vicar of course. The hall will look magnificent at that time of the year. Can I phone mum and tell her?"

"Of course, silly."

Saron was gushing on the phone to Lady Jervis and he heard Saron say don't cry Mum.

"Is she ok?"

"Yes, just a bit emotional though."

"Can I just ask one thing Saron?"

"What's that my darling?"

THE SORROW BEGINS

"You and your Mum do all the arranging please, that part does my head in."

"I know, of course we will."

He hugged her as their food arrived.

"Ooh lovely, thank you," Saron said to the young waiter.

It was 10.00pm when they left Castlegram for the Tow'd man. On arrival there were four holiday makers and three locals, and Tracey behind the bar. Saron shouted Tracey over. John went to the toilet.

"We have set a date, Tracey."

"What for?"

"The wedding silly."

"Oh yeah, sorry, miles away."

"When is it?"

"Christmas Day at the hall."

John Gammon Peak District Detective

"Oh, how lovely."

"Get a dress sorted, you will be invited."

"Thanks Saron, can I finish now?"

"Yes, I can sort these few and lock up, thanks Tracey."

Tracey glanced at John giving the look of 'unbelievable'. She grabbed her coat and left. John could sense she was one annoyed young lady.

"She was in a rush John, wasn't she?"

"Yes, but she starts early with the cleaning business I bet."

"Oh yeah, I forgot about that."

The customers all left by 11.30pm so John locked up and Saron went upstairs. He entered the bedroom and Saron was spread

THE SORROW BEGINS

on the bed in a cream basque with a blue trim, her long blonde hair cascading over her shoulders. They made love and it was almost 2.00am when they finally fell into each others' arms and went to sleep.

The following morning it had snowed even more. As John set off for Bixton he decided to take the main road knowing the back roads would possibly not be passable. On arrival Gammon organised a meeting in the incident room.

It was 9.00am.

"Good morning all. I just want a quick meeting to run though what we have now that we have two murders to sort."

Gammon pointed to the two dead people, Duncan Mule and Roger Thorndyke. Next to these were the suspects

John Gammon Peak District Detective

Robinson Spencer, Rod Goff, Phil Sterndale and Bobby Lint.

"Why Lint Sir?"

"Good question, Sergeant Magic."

"Yesterday I interviewed Gayle Thorndyke. During the interview it was clear that she and her husband were not a couple in the true sense. We already know Mr Thorndyke kept a Latvian girl in a flat in Bixton and was seeing her on occasions. Her name is Petra Silvu. He keeps her and pays the bills for sexual favours. This girl also works at the golf club. Mrs Thorndyke also was seeking companionship with one of our suspects, a Mr Bobby Lint. Bobby Lint is friends with these golfing cronies and they formed a consortium to buy the land that Phil Sterndale's parents owned.

THE SORROW BEGINS

They are now building five bedroomed properties on the land, but Thorndyke voted Bobby Lint out and he would not let him join the deal. Now this could have been because he knew Lint was screwing his wife, or he thought that Lint couldn't afford it coming from the council estate."

"I always thought Lint was punching above his weight John."

"I tend to agree with DI Lee."

"Right DI Scooper with DI Lee check Bobby Lint's back account."

"Yes Wally?"

"Don't you want to hear what I found with the body."

"Sorry Wally, fire away."

"Roger Thorndyke was being treated for a sexual transmitted disease, Gonorrhea or as you lot would know clap."

John Gammon Peak District Detective

There was some laughing in the room. "Gonorrhea is a sexual transmitted disease with the medical name Bacteria Neisseria Gonorrhea. Quite often men don't show any symptoms other than a burning sensation when urinating, they may have discharge also. This disease which in most cases is not life threatening, has killed seven hundred people infected by it in 2015. Mr Thorndyke's condition was very much in the advanced stage. I would suggest that both his wife and girlfriend should be made aware they must visit a doctor. Mr Thorndyke's body also showed sign of restraint similar to Mr Mule's body, so I would conclude they were into some kind of sexual game with somebody. Although Mr Thorndyke was strangled this

THE SORROW BEGINS

was not the cause of death. He died from heart failure or as we term it Congestive Cardiac Failure."

"Anything else Wally?"

"No, that's me done."

"Ok, well like I said Scooper and Lee get going on Bobby Lint's bank account and background. Sergeant Magic and DI Smarty look into Phil Sterndale's bank account and background, then do the same with Robinson Spencer. I will go and give the bad news to Petra Silvu and Gayle Thorndyke. Thanks everyone, 9.00am meeting tomorrow to discuss findings."

Gammon left the meeting and headed to Gayle Thorndyke's house. This could be a tricky one he thought as he drove to Riverside Mill, Dilley Dale. Maybe he

John Gammon Peak District Detective

should have brought Sandra along. Anyway, he was here now so needed to get on with it. Gayle was just leaving for work.

"Mr Gammon have you news of what happened?"

"Well I am afraid it looks like murder by strangulation although his heart gave out. I need to be honest with you, we are pretty sure Roger was into some sexual games."

Gayle laughed in like a nervous way.

"Roger, sexual games? I don't think so Mr Gammon."

"Well we have found marks on his body that relate to this sort of behaviour. The reason I am here is to tell you to get checked out at the doctors, because Mr Thorndyke had Gonorrhea. If you were

THE SORROW BEGINS

engaged in anything with Mr Thorndyke and Mr Lint then you need to be checked, and so does Mr Lint."

Gayle looked shocked. It was clear the revelations were not what she was expecting.

"It will be that slut he kept in Bixton, bloody trash," and she broke down.

Gammon thought Gayle Thorndyke was basically a good person and the shock had got to her. Gayle gathered herself then told Gammon she needed to get off to work. Gayle sped out of the drive and Gammon set off for Petra Silvu's place at Bixton.

Thorndyke hadn't exactly put the girl in an executive flat. Market Street in Bixton wasn't the best of areas of the town, and Petra had a one bedroom flat. Gammon knocked on the door. Petra came to the

John Gammon Peak District Detective

door. Through all the make up Gammon could see she was a pretty girl.

"Oh, hello Mr Gammon."

"Can I come in Petra?"

"Yes of course, excuse the mess." She was still in her dressing gown. As they walked in she was picking up underwear that was strewn round the floor. This girl wasn't loyal to Thorndyke it was obvious.

"Look I will be quick. Mr Thorndyke was found to have Gonorrhea when his body was investigated. So you need to visit a doctor urgently, and if you have had other sexual partners they need to do the same."

Petra looked confused.

"I am clean girl Mr Gammon."

"That's as maybe Petra, but you need to get checked out."

THE SORROW BEGINS

Gammon left Petra in shock, but he had done his bit he thought.

As Gammon got back in his Jaguar he felt a sharp pain run up his back and down his left leg. He knew what it was. It had happened three times lately, so maybe a visit to the doctors was in order? It was almost lunch time so John called at the Tow'd Man to see Saron.

"Hello John, what you doing here at this time? Are you missing me?"

"Of course I am. Just doing some work near by so thought I would have lunch with you."

"Ah that's nice, thank you. I know you don't want to hear about the wedding, but Mum as organized three marquees and we will get married at St John the Baptist

John Gammon Peak District Detective

church at Trissington. All the family going back hundreds of years have got married there. Mum is in her element. She is taking me wedding dress shopping on Saturday."

"Where are you going?"

"London to Francois Couvear."

"Isn't that the one that does all the Royal Families wedding dresses?"

"The very one. I know you won't understand but seeing that my mother is still a Lady it would be frowned upon not to go there, John. Mum is buying it, in fact she said she is paying for everything. Where shall we honeymoon, Maldives or somewhere?"

"Sweetheart until I have these cases put to bed, could we just have a weekend break in say Whitby?"

THE SORROW BEGINS

"Ok, I know you love your job Gammon. Now what do you want on your sandwich?"

"Just cheese and onion please."

"Coming up. So pleased you called."

John smiled.

With his lunch done and Saron happy that the wedding was progressing Gammon drove back to Bixton. DCI Cook met him on the stairs.

"John, I forgot to say I have two appointments in London this afternoon, and the morning. Then I am taking the rest of the week off. I have some friends in Greenwich so stopping with them for a few days."

"That's fine Ma'am," he said and carried on up to his office.

John Gammon Peak District Detective

Carl was back after his break and asked John if he could have a word in private.

"Of course, come in Carl."

John shut the office door behind him.

"What is it mate?"

"Beth, John I know she is alive. The guy who supposedly lived there for all those years has gone. The estate agent said he paid in full and he was only renting. I had a picture of Beth and showed it to the lady at the local newsagents. She said that this lady would come into the newsagent shop regularly and her name was Amy Baker. Although her hair colour was different that was the name she used in Cornwall when she was first on the run, John."

THE SORROW BEGINS

Gammon could see the excitement in Carl's eyes, but he didn't go along with him trying to find her. He thought if she had wanted finding she would have been in touch with him somehow.

"Look mate I think you would serve Beth better by letting sleeping dogs lie, don't you?"

"John, I am convinced it was no accident that I saw her, and why would she use that name? Only me and MI6 would know it."

"Ok look Carl, I don't want to build your hopes up, but I have contacts in MI6 etc. Maybe I can get a message to her if she is indeed alive?"

"Would you do that for me John?"

"I will, but like I say you might be disappointed if she doesn't want you involved. I will do my best, but it may take a few months."

John couldn't tell Carl it was his sister Fleur who could give him the information, and he never knew when she would be in contact. It was now almost 5.30pm and Gammon switched his laptop off and was getting ready to leave for the night when DI Scooper came in all excited.

"They've got him John."

"Who?"

"Clive Wiggledon. He was trying to fly from Schiphol Airport in Holland to America, it's believed he was heading for Columbia. He should be here in two day's time."

"Hey that's great news Sandra."

THE SORROW BEGINS

"Are we going to celebrate at The Spinning Jenny?"

"Be rude not too, who is still here?"

"Everyone, they are working on the stuff for tomorrow's meeting."

"Right gather them up, drinks are on me."

Gammon called DCI Cook to tell her the news on Wiggledon. She was over the moon. She said she expected this to come up at one of her meetings.

"Saved the day again," she said to John. "Tell the team I will pay for the food."

"Thanks very much Amanda."

"Think we have got a decent one there, John."

"Think you are right Sandra. Come on let's get off and have a good night."

John Gammon Peak District Detective

They arrived at the Spinning Jenny but before they started drinking John told them the bad news about Brian Lund. There was a mixture of annoyance, also the unbelievable fact that this man could get away with what he did, and will carry on doing.

"Don't let's spoil this. Tonight we have collared an important psychopath, so let's raise a glass to our endeavors."

"Evening Kev, drinks all round for my crew one for yourself. Can Doreen do some sandwiches and bowls of chips, and things like that for us?"

"Yes, not a problem John."

Di Smarty was talking to Carl and Magic. DI Lee spotted a relation, so he was

THE SORROW BEGINS

tied up with him. It just left Scooper and John together.

"So, marriage then?"

"Yeah it's time Sandra."

"I hope you are right John. You are not marrying material, are you?"

"Why do you say that?"

"Flippin' heck, do I have to spell it out?"

"I know, but I need to change Sandra."

All the time John was having the conversation he was remembering everything he had done wrong, and he decided he was really going to change.

"You ok John?"

"Yes, just lately I have been getting these sharp pains down my left leg and a hot pain up my back."

John Gammon Peak District Detective

"Have you made an appointment at the doctors?"

"Not yet, but I will."

"You know it's that bullet John. You have to go, this could cripple you."

"I know Sandra, but we have got so much on and DCI Cook seems to have a lot of meetings away from the station."

"That's not your problem, she is the DCI, you need to go and get checked out."

"Ok, I will make an appointment tomorrow."

"You better or I will be on your case. Ok, so what are we drinking now?"

"Well I'm on double brandies."

"That's it then two double brandies Mr Gammon."

THE SORROW BEGINS

CHAPTER SIX

It was always the case when they celebrated a big arrest that the team would get messy in the pub. Quite often DI Smarty and DI Lee would just have one drink and a sandwich and leave, but it was now 10.00pm and they were still in the party mood.

John stood talking to Doreen.

"Was the buffet ok? It was a bit short flippin' notice John."

"I know, sorry about that Doreen. It was late yesterday when Clive Wiggledon was arrested at the airport in Holland."

"Don't usually ask you, but what about Roger Thorndyke and Duncan Mule? I hear they are murders."

John Gammon Peak District Detective

"Correct they have both been filed as murders."

"I'll tell you what, there won't be many folks round here shedding a tear for either of those two. The bloody pair of them were shifty."

"What do you mean shifty?"

"They are crooks, you must know that. It must be fifteen years back when they were involved in something with that guy from Derby. You know the one that died caused you loads of grief."

"Who, Brian Lund?"

"Yes, Lund that's him."

"How were they involved with him?"

"Girls, that's all I know. But they reckon that Pamela Mule had to cough up almost a million quid."

THE SORROW BEGINS

"Really?"

"Not so hot you police boys, are you?"

"Well at the station I don't think anybody has been there more than about ten years. I think Di Trimble is probably the longest server."

"I didn't think John, until I read about Mule and then Thorndyke then it clicked. They reckon they somehow got mixed up with Lund and his mates hoping to make a fast buck, but they were out of their league. The rumours were they owed Lund almost a million pounds, and there were contracts out on them. So Pamela Mule paid them, her family, the Standings, are very wealthy."

"Wow, I didn't know this, thanks Doreen."

John Gammon Peak District Detective

"Anytime, just give me more notice next time you are throwing a party please."

Doreen wandered off leaving John with his thoughts. So now there was a connection to Lund again, but John wasn't sure what, if anything, he could do with Lund, as he seemed untouchable for some reason. It was almost 11.30pm and there was just Carl and John left having a final night cap with Kev.

"It's good to see you out and about Carl. You had a rough time when your young lady died, so it was nice to see you happy."

Carl shot John a glance. John knew why Carl was happy, he believed Beth to be alive. What a co-incidence for Kev to mention it.

THE SORROW BEGINS

"One for the gutter Kev?"

"What are you having?"

"Let's stick with the double brandies."
Kev brought the drinks back

"I hope you didn't mind me saying about Beth, Carl?"

"No that's fine Kev."

"Well you know how in life we say we all have doppelganger. Well your Beth has one, not same coloured hair but same figure and features. I saw her yesterday going into a cottage just outside Monkdale. I was going to Sheffield and took the scenic route. At Halleysop-on-le-dale. You know where the train used to go through, there is that one cottage with ivy growing up it. I think years ago, didn't Morag Slater live there? Now there was a character, Morag was one of seven sisters all their names began with

John Gammon Peak District Detective

M. There was Morag, she was the youngest, and the last survivor. Then there was Mandy, Margaret, Millie, Meredith, Myra and the eldest Maureen. They drank at Up The Steps Maggie's, but would come in here on darts night. Bet they would have a gallon a piece, and they did that every night."

John could see Carl wasn't listening to Kev. His mind was on the cottage and Beth.

"Bloody hell I could tell you some stories about the seven M's, as the locals called them. They never married, and eventually when the last one died the cottage was left to Maggie at Up The steps Maggie. I think she was good to Morag at the end. Maggie sold it a few years back. I

THE SORROW BEGINS

don't know who owns it now but it's' a bit out of the way."

"It certainly is Kev. I remember the M's they came to Pritwich Wakes, once a rum lot I'll tell you."

"You ok Carl? You have gone quiet."

"Think I best make a move, any chance of a room tonight?"

"You are both welcome Carl. I have nobody in at the minute. It's only five weeks to Christmas and folks start saving their money."

Carl went off to bed John and Kev had another drink then they hit the sack.

The following morning Carl was up and gone before John could speak with him. John had some toast and jam that Doreen had kindly made for him, then headed for

John Gammon Peak District Detective

work. John had called the meeting for 9.00am to go over what everyone had found.

Gammon entered the room and looking round could see no Carl.

"Who are we waiting on Dave? Is it just Carl?"

"No, he has phoned in sick about half an hour ago."

"More like a hangover."

"Don't judge Magic, we have all been there."

John knew where Carl would be. He would have gone to see if it really was Beth at Halleysop-on-le-dale.

"Ok, well let's crack on. Sandra and Peter what have you found?"

THE SORROW BEGINS

"Right, it appears Bobby Lint has two accounts, one with Lloyds bank, that one appears to be the account he uses to pay his bills etc. The other one is a joint account with a Mrs G Thorndyke."

"This is interesting Sandra."

"Well it could be. At the moment it's held in the Nat West in Jersey Channel Islands. We contacted the bank, but they are not willing to release any details of the joint account without the authority of the account holders, or something from our court to say we have authority. This has to be done in person."

"Right, we can talk about this after then."

"Dave, what have you and Magic found?"

John Gammon Peak District Detective

"Phil Sterndale has three accounts, a joint account with Mrs Sterndale, again this is generally bills, shopping fuel etc. His second account is in his name only that is with RBS in Micklock. We found quite a few strange transactions, not for very large amounts, but for between eighty pounds and two hundred and twenty pounds, this goes to three accounts; Sun and Sand, Lost Souls and a Miss Frokel. The problem we hit is Sun and Sand and Lost Souls. we are unable to trace. Miss Frokel has no address just a box number, and again we are unable to trace it."

"So, everyone thoughts please?"

"I would say Frokel is a mistress of some kind. The other two, not a clue."

THE SORROW BEGINS

"Well, at least you tried the room," he laughed leaving Sergeant Magic a bit red faced.

"Ok, now what about Robinson Spencer?"

"He appears to have one bank account that is constantly in the red and has been for almost four years. Other than that, nothing other than previous convictions which we know about."

"Ok DI Lee and Smarty."

"Right, now I am going to shock you. What I am about to tell you does not leave this room. If I find it has the person responsible will be bombed off the force immediately. Am I clear?"

They all nodded in agreement.

"Ok, well I have been visited by what I believe was two MI6 officers. Your friend

John Gammon Peak District Detective

and mine Mr Brian Lund is not dead. It was a put-up act, he has been sunning himself in Portugal. Apparently, he is a very high up informant. Derby City has got a major problem with drugs. Since Lund was made to disappear the Romanian mafia have moved in. So, the British Government has turned to this evil bastard to straighten it up whilst living under the protection of her Majesty's Government."

You could hear a pin drop. Everyone knew what Lund had done to Gammon's family, and they could not begin to think how he was feeling.

"Anyway, I found some local information out last night. The word has it that Mule and Thorndyke, a good few years ago, somehow got involved in some get rich

THE SORROW BEGINS

quick scheme with Lund and his cronies. They ended up with just short of a million pounds debt hanging over them. That is until Pamela Mule bailed them out. She is the daughter of Patrick Standing, yes you got it, the guy that was Governor of Hong Kong many years ago, and made his money in diamonds. Well she bailed her husband out and paid Lund to leave them alone. It is of no surprise to me that these killings have happened, and guess who is back in the saddle. Our friend Mr Brian Lund."

"So, this is what will happen. Myself and DI Scooper will fly to Jersey tomorrow to look into this bank account. DI Smarty and DI Lee you question Pamela Mule. Let's see what the connection was with Lund. Sergeant Magic I want you to stake out Bobby Lint. I want his every move

John Gammon Peak District Detective

documenting, where he goes, and who he sees. At some point in the very near future I want to raid Maggie Silito's farm at Hittington. She is clearly running some kind of sex service from there, but that can wait until I get back. Dave just get a warrant for the next few days' time mate."

"No problem John."

"Ok thanks everybody."

"Are you ok to go to Jersey tonight, Sandra?"

"Yes, no problem, Mum and Rosie have gone to see a cousin in Ireland."

"They like their trips out those two," and he laughed.

"Ok, well get off and get a bag packed. I'll sort out flights and letter of authority for

THE SORROW BEGINS

the bank. I best speak with Jersey police just out of protocol."

Sandra left to get an overnight bag. John booked the flights and spoke with the bank and organised the authority letter. He then called Amanda Cook.

Gammon nipped home calling Sandra on the way and said he would pick her up. They were flying at 5.30pm from East Midlands Airport. John picked Sandra up at 3.30pm. After the usual security check at the airport they boarded at 5.30pm for the one hour ten minutes flight to Jersey. The plane took off on time and they landed at St Peter Point. They picked up a hire car and drove to their hotel, The Mermaid.

John Gammon Peak District Detective

"Get freshened up Sandra and I'll meet you in reception at 8.00pm and we can have a meal in the restaurant."

John and Sandra headed for their rooms. John quickly phoned Saron to tell her where he was, but omitted to say he was with Sandra in case of any repercussions. Saron was fine with it, she understood his work having been in the police. She said she had a retirement party from Pippa's Frozen Foods in, so she would be late finishing anyway.

With everything sorted John showered shaved and put on his blue chinos with a cream shirt and blue Paul Smith jacket with tan coloured Kurt Geiger shoes. A quick splash of Givenchy Gentleman and John was ready. He headed down to reception

THE SORROW BEGINS

and enquired about a table for two for 8.40pm.

"Not a problem Sir, if you would like to have a drink in the bar once your friend arrives and I will bring some menus through for you."

Sandra arrived and looked stunning. She had a crème dress with a small brown shawl and brown shoes.

"Looking good Miss Scooper."

"Thank you, Mr Gammon."

"What would you like to drink?"

"I'll have a large Gin and Tonic, Hendrix if they have it, with a slice of cucumber please."

John ordered Sandra's request and a pint of Mary Anne Bitter himself.

"What a lovely hotel John."

John Gammon Peak District Detective

"Yes, I love the old ships beams and the paneling."

At spot on 8.40pm they were shown to their table. The restaurant was quite busy with a lot of mainly flambé dishes being served by chefs at the table.

The waiter was very attentive and explained they could have a normal meal or flambé.

"Let's go Flambé John."

The waiter gave them the flambé menu. John ordered a chewy red wine, as he called it, which Sandra took to me full bodied.

"Right, I know what I am having. Scallops, blood orange, salsify samphire and the steak Diane and shrimp scampi. What about you John?"

THE SORROW BEGINS

"I'll have the terrine of goose liver with a grape relish please, and moose with pistachio nuts flambé please. Do the dishes come with vegetables or do we order separate?"

"No Sir, all our meals come with the Mermaid garden vegetable selection."

They laughed and joked for the whole three hours of the meal which they both agreed was on par with the Spinning Jenny in Swinster.

"Let's go into the bar for a night cap."

A nice young lad was working the bar and it turned out he was from Ackbourne. His mother was a friend of Sandra's mother who did some charity work with her. They finished the brandies and John ordered a

John Gammon Peak District Detective

bottle of Moet et Chandon to take to the room.

"Where are you drinking that Mr Gammon?"

"I thought we could share it, either in my room or yours."

"I would feel better in mine."

"Yours it is then."

Sandra led the way. As John approached Sandra's room he did feel guilty. He had promised himself he would behave, and even told Sandra. He thought Sandra was out to prove a point. The room was plush and John opened the bubbly and poured Sandra's glass first.

"Mm that is certainly nice John."

John took a swig then made a move on Sandra.

THE SORROW BEGINS

"Whoa hold it there Mr Gammon, you are betrothed."

John thought she was joking.

"Look John I did this for a reason. Yes, I would like to sleep with you, but I'm not. It's not fair on Saron and not fair on you. If you truly love Saron then on Christmas Day you will be the happiest man alive, but if you can't commit your love and attention then please don't go ahead with it."

With that Sandra pecked him on the cheek and asked John to leave. John knew she was right but then Sandra usually was.

The following morning over breakfast John thanked Sandra for her honesty. They made their appointment at the Nat West with the bank manager, a Mr Hind. Hind checked the documents authorising Gammon and

John Gammon Peak District Detective

Scooper access to Bobby Lint and Gayle Thorndyke's joint account. There was almost seven hundred thousand pounds that appeared to have been put into the account over a period of fourteen months. There were varying amounts and it was always Gayle Thorndyke who deposited the money, sometimes electronically, sometimes at the bank in Micklock and a couple of times actually at the bank in Jersey.

Gammon thanked Mr Hind and left the bank with copies of the transactions. They had a couple of hours before their flight so they decided to have a ride round the island before dropping the hire car off at the airport and the flight home.

THE SORROW BEGINS

With the island being small they had soon been around the periphery. They stopped for a coffee at a small place in a cove. John was surprised it was still open with it being almost December because everything seemed shut-down.

"Two coffees and two blackberry tarts with custard please."

"Where are you from may I ask?"

"Derbyshire and you?"

"Well originally from Derbyshire myself, a place called Bixton."

"Really, we are police officers, our station is at Bixton."

"Well what a small world. I didn't really know anybody other than that guy who was a hairdresser and became a copper, Lee something."

John Gammon Peak District Detective

"Oh yes, Lee Hanney, he was our desk sergeant. I am afraid Lee is no longer with us."

"Mind it was a good few years ago and I haven't been back for twelve years. I've no family to speak of since Mum died."

"So, is this your place?"

"Yeah, I came over here working as a heating engineer, got married, got divorced, then bought this little place six years ago. Love the life, look at that view. I wake up to that every morning."

"You certainly are a lucky man. I'm John and this is Sandra."

"Oh sorry, should have introduced myself. I'm Dick Taylor."

"Pleased to meet you Dick."

THE SORROW BEGINS

"I best get your drinks and puddings, just nice to see fellow Peak District folk."

Dick went off to get the drinks.

"Small world eh, Sandra."

"Very much John, but I am not sure I believe his story. I am going to check him out when I get back."

"Flippin' heck, always on duty, eh Sandra."

They said goodbye to Dick Taylor and left the beautiful cove and headed for the airport. The flight was on time and they arrived back at Bixton police station at 3.50pm. John briefed Amanda Cook on what they had found at the Nat West in Jersey.

John Gammon Peak District Detective

Gammon checked with Smarty to see if he had the warrant for the Silito's farm the following day. He had and it was arranged for 9.00am. Gammon told Smarty he would meet everyone at 9.00am at the entrance to the farm. Gammon finished some paperwork. Amanda Cook had left and there was only Sandra in her office, so he stuck his head round the door to say goodnight.

"Hey John, come and look at this."
"What?"
"Dick Taylor, the guy we met at the café in Jersey."
"Yeah, what about him?"
"He is Gayle Thorneycroft's brother."

THE SORROW BEGINS

"Really, he said he didn't have family, didn't he?"

"Look, he was arrested sixteen years ago for misplacement of funds. He was a financial advisor, not a heating engineer."

"Are you sure it's him?"

"Sure I am, look I have a picture."

Without doubt it was him. He had darker hair back in the day, but there was no doubt the picture and Dick Taylor were the same man.

"Looking at some more records it looks like he was a bit of a tear-away in his youth. I know how he knew Hanney because Sergeant Hanney arrested him twice. Like I said, small world. I will keep digging John."

"Where are you off to?"

John Gammon Peak District Detective

"Just nipping to see Saron, then probably have a quick one with Kev at the Spinning Jenny. Pop in when you finish."

"Let me see how I go John."

"Goodnight then."

"Yeah goodnight John."

Sandra was too engrossed on Dick Taylor. She was like a dog with a bone when she thought she had something.

John arrived at the Tow'd Man. As usual Saron was busy in the kitchen.

"Hello sweetheart, how are you?"

"I'm good John, how was Jersey?"

"Yeah good, think we made a break through."

"We?"

"You know, the case."

THE SORROW BEGINS

"Oh, I see. Well I have some news for you."

"What's that?"

"I have two people who want to come into the pub with me."

"Not another set of nutters I hope?"

"No, Tracey Rodgers has sold her house in London. Her divorce is final and she has capital."

"Well I thought she had the cleaning business with Carol Lestar."

"She does, but apparently Carol's mum is going to America for some pioneering treatment, and Carol has to go with her. They can't afford to employ somebody with the business only just getting off the ground. So Tracey decided to ask me if I would be interested. I did what you said, and told her I would have to think about it.

John Gammon Peak District Detective

Then this afternoon I took a call from your old boss at Bixton."

"Who? I have had a few lately."

"Donna Fringe, her parents have passed away and she is an only child. All the sale of the house goes to Donna, and she sees this as a way out of the force."

"Wow that is a shock, I hadn't heard from Donna in ages."

"What do you think?"

"Well they would both be better than that clown previously. I don't know Tracey Rodgers too well, and only know Donna through work, not particularly socially. Think you should see them both and see what vision they have for the pub."

"Yes, I thought that John. What are you doing tonight?"

THE SORROW BEGINS

"Going to nip and have a quick drink with Kev. then an early night. I am knackered with all that travelling."

"Ok give me a ring tomorrow," Tracey said. "There is a trip going to see Elvis Sunday night at Bixton Opera House. Shall we see if we can go?"

"Yes, I'll ask Kev."

"Have you made that appointment to see the doctor?"

"Saron I have been busy."

"Shall I make it for you?"

"If you want."

"Ok, I will call tomorrow and let you know."

"Ok, good night Miss Nag,"

Saron laughed kissed John and he left.

John Gammon Peak District Detective

It was 7.20pm and John called at the Spinning Jenny.

"Hi Kev, do you think Doreen will do me a take away for 9.00pm?"

"I would say so lad. What's up, with you leaving early?"

"Just a lot on and been burning the candle at both ends lately."

"Ok, mate what would you like?"

"Just Derbyshire bangers and mash with onion gravy and veg please mate."

"Do you want me to ask her for a few roast potatoes and a Yorkshire pudding?"

"If you think she will do it mate?"

"You are the only one who could get away with it lad, she treats you like a son," and Kev chuckled making his red dickie bow bounce up and down.

THE SORROW BEGINS

Kev returned and started pulling John his pint of Pedigree.

"Big night tonight, John."

"Why is that mate?"

"It's the Spinning Jenny weigh-in mate."

"What's that?"

"Well Doreen was talking to Shelly and the crew. They were on about going to that weight watchers thing, but we said they could do it here."

"So, who is weighing in?"

"Doreen, me, Jack, Shelley, Cheryl, Bob and I think Steve and Jo were on about coming if Tracey would baby-sit."

"So, who is keeping the records?"

"Sheba Filey, she is discreet but I am sure weights will get out."

John Gammon Peak District Detective

"Can't wait for next week when they start comparing Kev," John laughed.

At 8.00pm they trooped in. Kev went down first and came back up looking sheepish.

"How did you do mate?"

"I reckon these scales are wrong. I'm never seventeen stone four pounds."

John almost choked on his beer. Next up was Jack, he came out beaming.

"Twelve stone twelve pound, I haven't been that weight since I was forty, Kev."

Bob was next and he was happy. Doreen was ok. Cheryl was heavier because Bob had been to Bruges with work and brought back chocolates, so it was his fault. Shelley said she was ok.

"Doesn't look like Steve and Jo are coming."

THE SORROW BEGINS

Doreen had no sooner got the words out of her mouth when they walked in.

"Sorry about that, the little one was getting upset before we left."

Jo went first and said she was happy. Steve came up blaming Jo that she had to stop making apple and blackberry crumble.

"I don't make him eat it Doreen."

John could not believe how entertaining this was and he could see the potential for even more laughs as the weeks go on.

"While I have got you all, I need your money for the tickets and bus for the Elvis impersonator night at Bixton Opera House on Sunday?"

John Gammon Peak District Detective

"It's ok John, Saron called and paid me. Sheba said she was going but she might be bringing a friend, so she paid for two."

John was intrigued and Sheba knew he was, so she avoided him just to aggravate him.

John left with his dinner at 9.00pm much to the amazement of the gang. On his way down Hittington Dale he saw a majestic stag standing in one of the fields. With the full moon lighting everywhere and it being a crisp cold night he stood out. John was thinking it was one of those times where you wished you had a camera. He finally arrived at his cottage, everywhere seemed peaceful. John made himself a coffee, put on his North Face puffa jacket and took his coffee into the garden. Quite often he had

THE SORROW BEGINS

seen a badger making its way across the bottom of the garden and tonight was no exception.

John sat reflecting on life. He was pleased Sandra had knocked him back, but concerned he was too weak and would have given in. Saron was beautiful, everyman's dream. She dressed well, she looked great and had a super personality. What more could he want?

It was almost 11.20pm when a fox and her cubs came across the garden. The fox stopped when she saw John sitting at the garden table. She stared at John for a good few minutes before chastising her cubs and carrying on their journey.

John Gammon Peak District Detective

What was he going to do about Carl? From everything Carl had said it seemed likely it was Beth. He wished Fleur would make contact, she would know.

Realising the time John took his coffee cup and rinsed it in the sink and headed for bed.

The alarm went off at 7.30am as usual. Normally John was awake before it but this morning he was sound asleep, so it woke him up with a start. He quickly shaved and showered and headed for Beryl's Butties for their famous bacon sandwich. He knew today was going to be a long day.

The café was quite full with truck drivers and builders on their way to work. John stood out in a suit, but it was worth it he thought to have a Beryl's doorstep bacon

THE SORROW BEGINS

buttie. John finished his sandwich paid, and headed for the search at Maggie Silito's farm.

John Gammon Peak District Detective

CHAPTER SEVEN

As he approached he could see a lot of police at the gateway at the top of the drive. Gammon wanted to execute the warrant himself. It was, without doubt, a beautiful set of buildings and no way could Silito afford this on a bar manager's wage at Bixton Golf Club. John knocked loudly on the oak door of the main house. At first there was no answer but eventually Silito answered. She was dressed in a silk dressing gown, the type you see oriental women wearing. Silito looked shocked at the amount of police presence.

"Margaret Silito I have warrant to search these premises."

THE SORROW BEGINS

Maggie Silito tried to protest but they breezed past her. Gammon sent Scooper and Milton to the barns with Smarty. DI Lee, Gammon and Magic searched the house. The first door Gammon opened was a bedroom. Trying to get dressed was Alec Blake one of the consortium from the golf club.

"Well, well, Mr Blake, going somewhere are we?"

Blake was only half dressed.

"DI Lee, I want to question Mr Blake. Let him get dressed then take him to the station, I will be along shortly."

Silito was complaining to anyone who would listen that this was police harassment. They went through the rest of the house finding very little, so Gammon

John Gammon Peak District Detective

and Sergeant Magic headed for the barns. DI Smarty met Gammon. Now Smarty had quite a sense of humour and he was trying not to laugh. He explained that in the first bedroom they had found Iman Oglee dressed in all leather whipping Freddie Slack.

"I have to see this Dave."

Gammon went in. Freddie Slack was tied to the bed trying to plead his innocence. Iman just stood looking down.

"Ok Dave arrest them both and take them to Bixton."

Smarty gestured to two constables.

"Tell them they can have a solicitor if they wish."

THE SORROW BEGINS

The young constable nodded to say he understood.

"Anything else Dave?"

"Oh yeah, wait for this one."

Dave opened the door. The room had the full torture chamber in it.

"Carry on searching please Carl with Sandra, and we will go back and interview this lot."

Gammon and Smarty headed back to Bixton both in fits of laughter.

"Did you expect this John?"

"I expected something, but Freddie Slack was a pure bonus."

They arrived back

"Ok Sergeant Yap, where are they all?"

John Gammon Peak District Detective

Sergeant Yap was trying to keep a straight face.

"Interview room one is Maggie Silito and her solicitor. Room two is Iman Oglee. Three is Freddie Slack. Four is Alec Blake."

"We might as will start at interview room one and Maggie Silito."

"Oh before you do sir, Silito and Iman Oglee are using the same solicitor."

"Ok thanks Ian."

A young PC started the tape running as Gammon and Smarty entered the room, stating date time and who was present.

THE SORROW BEGINS

"Ok Ms Silito, I have a few questions for you. Do you know why I arrested you today?"

"No comment," she replied.

"Well I arrested you for running a house of ill repute. Are you the Madam of the establishment?"

"No comment."

"You see Maggie, can I call you Maggie?"

Silito nodded.

"I always have a problem with interviewees who want to just say 'no comment'. It makes me uneasy like they are trying to hide something."

"My client has the right to remain silent if she wishes DI Gammon."

"Correct Mr Saul, but it doesn't help our investigation. Let me explain I have two

John Gammon Peak District Detective

dead bodies that are currently both unsolved crimes. On investigation into both deaths it was clear that both men had engaged in some kind of sexual gratification with pain involved. I am not knowledgeable in these practices but both men were found strangled. They both had laceration on their backs consistent with being lightly whipped. They also had shoe heel marks. I would like to ask Ms Silito how she thinks these came about?"

"No comment," Maggie said once again.

"Ok, let see if you can help me, then I will see if I can help you. Did Mr Duncan Mule or Mr Thorndyke ever visit your establishment?"

THE SORROW BEGINS

Silito whispered to her lawyer then replied, "No."

"So, the two men never came to the farm is that correct?"

"Correct," she said.

"If you are purposely being obstructive in our murder investigations this could carry a jail sentence. So, to make it very clear, Duncan Mule or Roger Thorndyke, two customers you serve at Bixton golf club, have never been to your establishment?"

"No, they have never been to where I live."

"Can I just re-iterate for the tape where you live is being used as a brothel."

"You are jumping to conclusions there Mr Gammon."

John Gammon Peak District Detective

"Mr Saul, are the rooms at your home equipped with torture chambers common to a brothel?"

"Well no, of course not."

"So why would your clients home be like this?"

"What people do in their homes is their business Mr Gammon."

"Well I am making it my business in Ms Silito's case. I will be holding your client for a further twenty four hours until the other people that were at Ms Silito's have been questioned, and I am satisfied the truth is being told."

"Take Ms Silito to the holding cell please, DI Smarty."

THE SORROW BEGINS

"Mr Gammon, I am representing Miss Iman Oglee as her solicitor also. Would it be possible to see her next?"

Gammon looked at Saul and smiled.

"I'm sorry, we will call you when we are ready. There is a break room if you need a drink Mr Saul."

Saul knew that Gammon was playing the game.

DI Smarty came back and next up was Freddie Slack. The tape was set up and Gammon and Smarty introduced themselves to Richard Jessop. Jessop was a renowned lawyer from Manchester. Gammon knew of his work. They always said if you want to get off with something then Tricky Dicky Jessop was your man.

John Gammon Peak District Detective

"Ok Mr Slack, ok if I call you Freddie?"

"By all means," Slack said in a confident and cocky manner.

"So today we raided a farm that we believed to be a house of ill repute. The reason was we have two unsolved murder cases and we believe there could be a connection. So, Mr Slack would you like to explain how you came to be there today and the reason you were tied up?"

"Yes, not a problem Mr Gammon, for the good of my back."

"For the good of your back? Please do explain Freddie?"

"Well some years ago me and one of my best friends were in a helicopter crash. Luckily he was ok, but I have had severe

THE SORROW BEGINS

back pain for many years. Anyway, I read somewhere that massage and things like light whipping would get the blood to the muscles, and it does. I was telling Iman at the golf club and she said she could sort it. Her place was too small, but Maggie would let her use her place."

"So, you can see my client is innocent of any charges you may want to level against him. If anything, I believe he is due an apology from Bixton constabulary," Richard Jessop said.

Gammon was annoyed, but he knew this guy was a really good lawyer.

"For the record I would like to say, whilst I can't prove that you attended a brothel, we will be monitoring the situation, Mr Slack. Should we find evidence that Margaret Silito has been running a house of ill-repute we may ask you back for further interviews. Good day to you."

"Ok Dave, let's interview Alec Blake."

Gammon and Smarty entered Interview room four. The young PC started the tape running and Blake's solicitor, a Mr South, introduced himself.

"Mr Blake, I have a few questions for you."

Blake nodded.

"Do you pay Ms Silito for her services?"

"No," Blake answered.

"Then what were you doing there?"

"Enjoying myself, is that a crime?"

"No enjoyment isn't a crime, but paying for that type of enjoyment is I am

THE SORROW BEGINS

afraid. How long have you known Ms Silito?"

"A long time."

"Have you been to her house before?"

Slake had no shame about answering Gammon's questions.

"Many times, she is a friend."

"Is that a friend with benefits then Mr Blake?"

"I'm sorry Mr Gammon, but I find your line of questioning downright intrusive," said Blake's solicitor.

"Well let me tell you something, Mr South."

"I am investigating two murders on my patch, both friends of Mr Blake. They showed signs of some kind of sexual gratification, and one had a sexual transmitted disease. I would suggest your

John Gammon Peak District Detective

client get himself checked out. What I will say is, I think your client is lying, but for that I need proof so he is free to go."

"But be aware Mr Blake, you are under my scrutiny until these murders are resolved. Good day to you."

South and Blake left. Gammon turned to Smarty.

"Not having much luck, are we Dave?"

"Let's see what Iman Oglee has to say for herself."

Gammon told the young PC to start the tape.

"Well Iman, you have two jobs?"

"No just one job at golf club, Mr Gammon."

"So how do you explain your dress sense?"

THE SORROW BEGINS

"I was having fun."

"Were you paid for having fun?"

"No, absolutely not Mr Gammon."

"You do know we are investigating the murders of two people you knew, don't you Iman?"

Iman nodded.

"For the tape, Miss Oglee nodded in agreement to my question. With this in mind Iman, if you are holding out on any information that might hinder our enquiries to the two men then there is a likelihood you could be deported or jailed. Do I make myself clear?"

Iman again nodded she understood, and Gammon reiterated it for the tape.

"Ok Miss Oglee, you are free to leave, but you may be questioned again if any new evidence comes to light."

John Gammon Peak District Detective

Iman and her solicitor got up and left.

"Well that was a bloody waste of time Dave."

"Well at least we ruffled a few feathers."

"Ok mate, let Silito go, we have no case."

With it being the weekend and Friday night now upon them John left work and headed to the Tow'd Man. It was a really cold Derbyshire night. So John took it steady as he headed for the Tow'd Man down the back routes from Bixton. The Tow'd Man stood alone and from a distant John imagined how this former coaching inn must have looked a like an oasis from a distance to a weary traveler in a coach coming from York on their way to London.

THE SORROW BEGINS

It was almost 6.30pm when John arrived so he headed for the kitchen and Saron.

"Hey John, I am so excited. I interviewed Donna Fringe and have decided to take her offer. She will start first week of December."

"Well I am pleased. Donna is a really nice person, I would trust her."

"While you are here, I have picked out a wedding dress and me and mum are going to look at it next week."

"Do you want me to sort the honeymoon?"

"I'm not pushing John, but it will be here before we know it."

"Like I said I would prefer a few days in the UK with the current situation at work. Then later on in the year perhaps we

John Gammon Peak District Detective

could do a really nice holiday like the Maldives, or I would like to see the Galapagos Islands."

"Oh, that sounds great John. We have to see the vicar at Trissington Church next week to get things like flowers arranged and ushers etc. Don't panic, me and mum can do it."

John smiled.

"Oh John, I am so happy and can't believe it is finally going to happen for us."

"What time will you be finished tonight Saron?"

"It's going to be late, about 10.30pm. I want to get a load of prep done with going to Bixton Opera House on Sunday night."

"Oh crap, I forgot about that."

"John what are you like?"

THE SORROW BEGINS

"Ok, well I may as well have a pint with Kev and an early night. I might be going into work tomorrow to catch up on paperwork."

"Are you stopping tomorrow night?"

"Yes, can do sweetheart."

"Ok come here," and Saron planted a big kiss on John. "Have a nice night and think of me slaving away. Roll on Donna coming."

"Have you told Tracey Rodgers?"

"Yeah, she wasn't too pleased John."

"She'll get over it."

John left for the Spinning Jenny. Kev was his usual dapper self; white shirt, red dickie bow that he had made his trademark look.

"Hello lad, how are you are you? Ready for Sunday night?"

John Gammon Peak District Detective

"Yes, we are looking forward to it. Have you filled the bus?"

"Yes, fourteen seater, I'm so pleased about that."

"Who's going?"

"Me and Doreen, you and Saron, Bob and Cheryl, Jack and Shelley, Carol Lestar and Tracey Rodgers, Sheba and somebody apparently, and Rita and Tony Sheriff from The Sycamore at Pritwich."

"That will be good, not seen Tony and Rita in ages. What time we setting off mate?"

"7.00pm sharp from here. He is supposed to be really good apparently he played with the Jordanaires Elvis backing group in Vegas, and they said he is the nearest thing to the man."

THE SORROW BEGINS

"Can't get a better praise than that mate."

"Right, what you having lad, Pedigree?"

"Yes please mate. Will Doreen do me a take away?"

"Told you before, you are the only person she would do it for John."

"I'll just have cottage pie with chips and peas for 8.45pm mate, if that's ok?"

Kev went of to tell Doreen and John took a sip from his beer. By the time he got back John was half-way down his pint and his phone rang.

"Evening Sir, sorry to bother you. Di Trimble here. I have had a call from Micklock police. They have a Philip Sterndale in custody who says he wants to speak with Detective Inspector Gammon."

John Gammon Peak District Detective

"Did they say what it was about Di?"

"No, they just said it maybe of interest to you."

"Ok Di, I will pop down."

"Kev, I'm sorry mate, duty calls. Can you cancel that order with Doreen? I have to go back in."

"You know how to get me in trouble lad."

"Sorry Kev, I will buy you a beer on Sunday."

Kev muttered something as John was leaving knowing he had to face the wrath of Doreen!

John arrived at Micklock station. It wasn't as big as Bixton and the building was a lot

THE SORROW BEGINS

older. It was only manned by a handful of officers.

"Evening, DI Gammon," and John showed his warrant card to the desk sergeant.

"How can I help you Sir?"

"I was told you had a Philip Sterndale in custody and he wanted to speak with me."

"Oh, just a moment Sir, DC Woods was handling that."

Gammon stood waiting when a DC Woods approached him. Woods was in his early forties with grey hair swept back revealing a receding hairline.

"DI Gammon," and Woods put out his hand to shake Gammon's hand.

"Pleased to meet you Sir, heard a lot about you."

John Gammon Peak District Detective

"All good I hope, DC Woods?"

"Absolutely Sir."

"Right what did you want?"

"I apprehended a Mr Philip Sterndale tonight."

"What for?"

"Well it all started quite normally. Me and the wife had been out for a meal when I saw an altercation across the road near Iceland in the town centre. I told my wife to wait where we were and I went over. Both men had blood on their faces. When I intervened and said I was a police officer one of the men ran off leaving just Sterndale."

"So how does that involve me DC Woods?"

THE SORROW BEGINS

"Well Sir. I took Sterndale to Micklock station and sent the wife home. I then interviewed Sterndale. At first he wasn't very co-operative, but when I asked who the other man was, he said he would only speak with you, as it was information about a case you were handling out of Bixton. So I thought I best call you."

"Ok DC Woods, show me where he is."

Gammon entered the interview room. Philip Sterndale was sitting with his head in his hands. His face had some bruising and there was dried blood on his knuckles.

"Mr Sterndale, it looks like you have been in the war. I believe you had something to tell me."

"Yes, I do. I had been for a pint at the Galloping Major in Micklock. I always go Friday night and get a taxi back to

John Gammon Peak District Detective

Hittington. He picks me up at the bus station, I always enjoy that five minute walk from the pub to the taxi rank. We get a few down us so it just clears my head a bit. Anyway, I just got by Iceland when from nowhere this guy appears with a base-ball bat and tries to hit me. I'm no slouch Mr Gammon and I managed to disarm him. I recognised his face, and he said he had a message from them to keep my big mouth shut, or next time it won't be a base-ball bat. By now that copper was approaching, and this dick head runs off."

"So, who are 'them' Mr Sterndale?"

"That bloody consortium that swindled our family out of the house and land."

"You got payment for it, Mr Sterndale."

THE SORROW BEGINS

"Aye, but not what it was worth Mr Gammon."

"So, you have been warned not to talk to the police. What exactly do you know Mr Sterndale?"

Sterndale took a long hard look at Gammon before saying, "Forget it."

"You drag me down here because you have an altercation, that's it?"

"Look Gammon, leave it, I will sort myself."

"Mr Sterndale, I can't stress the point enough, if you are being threatened, do not take the law into your own hands. That's what we are here for. Do I make myself clear?"

Sterndale nodded.

Gammon left the room and thanked DC Woods.

John Gammon Peak District Detective

"Was it any good for you Sir?"

"Not tonight but it's given ne food for thought, DC Woods. Thanks for getting in touch. Are you charging him?"

"No, I will caution him, not worth wasting our time on Sir."

John drove back and was just approaching the farm when the Hittington Church bell tower rang out for midnight. John closed the door behind him in the cottage, and was tempted to try a Jameson for a night cap. But knew that would end up more than one, and he had decided to do a fifteen mile walk the following day.

John was showered and ready to set off by 7.30am Saturday morning. He had a quick

THE SORROW BEGINS

word with Roger Glazeback and headed up the small peak towards Little Elf Wood, so called because legend had it that Malik an elf lived in the woods. He didn't want people walking there so he would frighten them so they kept away. Of course it was all myths and legends, but John had always been on edge right from a little boy because of the stories that surrounded Malik and the woods. John made his way as quickly as possible through the well trodden paths. That eventually brought him out near the farm where Adam's girl and the rest were slaughtered, at the so called safe house, by Lund's henchmen. The farm was called Field House Lockwood Farm and John stood at the top of Lead Lane which led down to the farm. Gosney was a very small

John Gammon Peak District Detective

hamlet perhaps even too small to call a hamlet.

Memories came flooding back, days when he would play with Billy Lockwood, and then the tragic day when Elle and Chris Gregory a good friend and protection officer, both died. Then he thought about the out buildings where ex-constable Sam Much and his wife had been slaughtered. Sam was still alive when John found him, but died in his arms. A very sad day John thought as he walked away. He could not believe the stupidity of the British Government for protecting Brian Lund.

John decided he mustn't dwell on it what was done was done, and he was going to enjoy the walk. John followed a dirt track

THE SORROW BEGINS

that passed alongside Sheba Filey's beautiful place. There was no sign of Sheba. John again climbed up the steep hill towards the main road, which he had to cross for the next part of the walk. John went down the side of a limestone wall eventually arriving at the Wrigley Tin Café. The Wrigley Tin was so called because it was clad on the sides and the roof with tin sheets. It was a popular spot for breakfast in the Peak District.

It was 9.30am and John found a seat in the corner next to the large cast iron stove that was belting heat out. A young girl came to take his order.

"What would you like Sir?"

John knew exactly what he wanted.

John Gammon Peak District Detective

"I'll have the full Wrigley Tin Belt Buster please."

"Would you like fried bread or toast with that Sir?"

"Fried bread please," John replied.

"And what would you like on your pancake stack?"

"What do you have?"

"All the pancakes come with cream Sir, and we have strawberry banana pancakes, double blueberry pancakes, New York cheesecake pancakes or just our buttermilk pancakes."

John was starving having not eaten the night before because of the visit to Micklock so was ready for feast.

"I'll have the New York cheesecake pancakes and a black coffee."

THE SORROW BEGINS

The Wrigley Tin always brought a big coffee pot out so you could have as much as you wanted. Very American was how the café was run. The guy who had bought it from the previous owner was an American who had married a local girl some ten years ago. When the café came up for sale about eighteen months ago they jumped at it. The menu was run as an English breakfast café with an American twist. The service was excellent as the young girl first brought out John's coffee pot followed by a massive breakfast plate. He had two sausages, two bacon slices, two eggs, black pudding, beans, tomatoes, mushrooms, fried potato and two slices of fried bread. Then another plate arrived with his New York cheesecake pancakes. John was starting to think he was being greedy, but looking round everybody

John Gammon Peak District Detective

was having the same. John had a good appetite especially as it had been almost twenty hours since he last ate, but even he was under pressure. He finished the breakfast but only managed three of the pancakes before he had to wave the white surrender flag that each table had to alert the waiter to bring the bill and take away the plates. John paid his bill which was only £7.80 for the breakfast and £1.50 for the coffee, it was an absolute bargain.

Now for the walk back he thought although he was going on a slight detour. John thanked the owners and placed three pounds in the staff tip box before setting off. The meal was laying heavy as he climbed to the top of Maurice Mole's Peak, another thing

THE SORROW BEGINS

from his childhood. His mother always said that legend had it that if you climbed Maurice Mole's Peak on the last Saturday of the month and took a mirror with you would get a reflection of the person you would marry. John's mum was full of myths and legends. He missed her greatly. From Mole's peak John headed down in the valley crossing across the well-worn stones in the low river of Pigeon Dale.

Once on the other side he stopped to chat with an elderly couple who said they had seen a common buzzard further down the valley. They were sat eating a sandwich with a cup of coffee and they said the buzzard had circled just to the right of them for almost three minutes, before diving at great speed to pick up what looked like a vole. They said it happened so quickly they couldn't be sure of the vole.

"We are so lucky to have this on our doorstep," the lady said as they strode off in the opposite direction.

John walked for about a further two miles down Pigeon Dale before having to start his ascent to Hittington. It was almost 4.00pm when John arrived back at the cottage. The hot shower was a welcome relief, he looked forward to it after a long walk.

He was cleaned up and settled down for the night to watch a film. John woke with a start it was 2.00am and the heating had gone off. The settee was now a cold place so he rushed upstairs to get under the duvet.

THE SORROW BEGINS

CHAPTER EIGHT

Sunday was a quiet day. John spent some time looking at short break for the honeymoon. He knew Saron would sort, but he wanted to show interest. The reality was, like all men, he wasn't into the preparation. He smiled to himself has he remembered an old DCI he had worked under in London. Greg Cameron was a grumpy guy in his late fifties who hated his job and couldn't wait to retire. If you asked a question in the incident room he would bark at whoever asked the question. 'I don't want the labour pains, just give me the baby', and that is how John felt about the pre-wedding preparation. He knew also Steve would have something lined up that would make him cringe on his stag night, so he wasn't particularly looking forward to that.

John headed for the Tow'd Man to pick Saron up. It was 6.30pm when he arrived to find Saron still in her chef gear.

"You will need to hurry up Saron, or we will miss the bus from the Spinning Jenny."

"I'm sorry John I can't come."

"Why not?" John said feeling aggrieved.

"I have a party of sixty fly fisherman coming and had arranged for staff. Neither the bar person or the chef have turned up. I have rung and rung the agency, but nobody is answering."

THE SORROW BEGINS

"What time should they have been here?"

"The chef was coming at 2.00pm to help prepare the buffet and the bar person at 5.00pm so I could show her the till etc."

"I am still doing the buffet, and I have asked Donna if she can start tonight instead of tomorrow. She should be here in about five minutes so I can help her."

"This bloody place, it winds me up Saron."

"Look John, it's no different to you letting me down with your job. I don't kick off like you."

John stormed out.

"I will call you tomorrow," he shouted as he left.

Feeling annoyed that again he wasn't going out with Saron he headed for the

Spinning Jenny. They were all on the car park as John pulled up.

"Where is she then lad?"

"Crisis at the pub, she can't make it mate."

"Oh, that's a shame John."

"It is what it is, Doreen, nothing I can do about it."

"I'm afraid that's the pub game John. Is it right your old DCI is going into partnership with Saron?"

John thought it was going to be a bit awkward for Tracey Rodgers. She was just getting on the bus so John waited a split second before answering.

"Yes, she is starting tonight instead of tomorrow because Saron has been let down by the agency."

THE SORROW BEGINS

"Nowt like being thrown in at the deep end lad."

"True Kev."

The bus set off.

Carol Lestar was a bit sheepish but as they were getting off she said she was flying out with her Mum the following day, and she pecked John on the cheek. Funny John thought, how much pleasure you get from helping people.
Bixton Opera House it was built in 1903 and designed by the same man who designed the London palladium. It was a quaint place with a couple of small rooms that had been turned into bars. You could get a drink and take it to your seat, quite a rare thing these days. They had a couple before a bell sounded which meant the

John Gammon Peak District Detective

Elvis impersonator would be on stage in five minutes, so everyone had to take their seats.

John was sat next to Shelley. It made John smile as sections of the audience had really dressed for the occasion, and it was like they were seeing the real Elvis.

The guy came on in a sequined white jump suit and Shelley commented how like Elvis he was.

"Good evening ladies and gentlemen," he said in a southern drawl.

"I am your Elvis tonight," and with that he broke into Jailhouse Rock.

John could not believe everybody was up dancing and women were screaming. By the end of the first act John was beginning

THE SORROW BEGINS

to think this was a mistake, he wasn't a big Elvis fan. He had just thought it would have given Saron a break from the pub. During the break Tracey Rodgers made a bee line for John.

"So where is the lovely Saron? Did she tell you she turned down my partnership request?"

"She mentioned it, but it's nothing to do with me Tracey."

"So what day you getting married Mr G?"

"Christmas Day, you will be invited. Just the invites haven't gone out yet."

Tracey looked at him in a sultry manner, then turned and ordered four double brandies. John didn't take much notice until she pointed to two of them and said, "They are yours, bottoms up."

John Gammon Peak District Detective

She downed both of hers, so John had little choice but to do the same. As he put his glass on the bar she had ordered another one each for them to take to the seats because the bell had rung to announce Elvis was back on stage. He did quite a lot of rock songs to which everybody danced. Then he said he was going to go slow for a few, and he started to sing the Wonder of You. Tracey grabbed John and had him dance with her. Luckily that got Jack and Shelley, Bob and Cheryl and the others up so he didn't feel so much on show.

"Stay with me tonight John," she said as she pushed her body against him. This was going to be hard to turn down John thought. Tracey dropped a key into John's pocket.

THE SORROW BEGINS

"Nobody will know John."

When the night ended the whole place were standing for Elvis. John thought it was ok, but he wouldn't go again. They made their way back onto the mini bus. Doreen said if they didn't mind, her and Kev were going straight to bed so no late drink at the Spinning Jenny. The bus dropped Tracey off on the way back. John, Carol, Doreen and Kev were taken back to the Spinning Jenny car park. John said good night and set off, but his weakness got the better of him and he headed to Tracey Rodger's place.

John parked round the back and let himself in. There were candles everywhere and a bottle of champagne on the table but no sign of Tracey.

John Gammon Peak District Detective

John sat at the table and he heard Tracey come downstairs. She had dressed for the occasion, John looked and had to pick his chin up off the floor.

She wandered over.

"You came then, I knew you would Mr G."

Tracey wrapped her arms round John and began passionately kissing him.

"Take me upstairs John."

John scooped her up and carried her to the bedroom. Their sexual fling lasted almost one and a half hours before finally they fell back on the bed exhausted.

They were both went silent for a few minutes before Tracey said "You won't

THE SORROW BEGINS

marry Saron. I know you won't, you only think you love her John."

"Look Tracey this was a one off."

"Oh, like the last time and I don't know how many countless times before."

John didn't have an answer, but he did know he would marry Saron, and he knew once they were married all this would stop.

The following morning John left at 7.30am. he kissed Tracey and smiled as he left.

John got to his cottage, showered and shaved then left for Bixton. On the way John called the station and told DCI Amanda Cook to get Gayle Thorneycroft and her solicitor in for further questioning about her brother Dick Taylor, the guy he and Sandra had met on Jersey.

John Gammon Peak District Detective

John arrived at the station and Sergeant Yap said Mrs. Thorneycroft and her solicitor would be at the station for 9.15am.

"Ok Sergeant Yap, when they arrive put them in interview room one and give me a shout."

Gammon grabbed his obligatory cup of dishwater as he called it and said hello to Amanda Cook. He headed for his office and the pile of paperwork waiting for him. Gammon was halfway through the pile when Sergeant Yap said he had put Gayle and her solicitor in interview room one. Gammon shouted DI Scooper to accompany him.

"Scooper, set the tape going."

"Good morning Gayle. Good morning Mr?"

THE SORROW BEGINS

"Bradshaw of Bradshaw and Bradbury. What is this about Mr Gammon?"

"Do you have a brother Gayle?"

"Yes, I do Mr Gammon. why?"

"Does your brother run a beach café in Jersey?"

Gayle waited a few seconds before answering.

"Yes, my brother Richard lives there, sorry he likes to be called Dick. Why Mr Gammon?"

"Just myself and DI Scooper had the need to visit Jersey, and we bumped into him at his café."

"Is that a crime DI Gammon?"

"No, it isn't Mr Bradshaw, but depending on how your client answers this next question, then we could have a crime."

Gayle looked at Gammon.

John Gammon Peak District Detective

"What do you mean Mr Gammon?"

"Can you tell me Gayle why you have an off-shore account in Jersey with a certain Mr Bobby Lint?"

Gayle became upset.

"I can't tell you Mr Gammon."

"The account has over seven hundred thousand pounds, that have been deposited over the last fourteen months. That is a large amount of money Gayle, and certainly not to be sniffed at. I would consider Mr Lint would not have that kind of money."

"I am sorry Mr Gammon, I truly can't say."

"I am disappointed Gayle, I saw you as an honest decent person. If for any reason this money is not legitimate, and has anything to do with the current murder

THE SORROW BEGINS

investigations you could be in serious trouble. Gayle, am I clear?"

"Yes, I understand Mr Gammon."

"Ok interview ended."

Gayle got up and shot a glance at Gammon, the kind that said I am wrong but I can't do anything about it.

Thorndyke and her solicitor left and Scooper turned to Gammon.

"Are we going to get Bobby Lint in for questioning?"

"No point Sandra. I think Gayle is spooked enough that things will start falling into place. We just have to be patient I think."

"Sir, DCI Cook would like a word."

"Ok Sergeant Yap, I am on my way upstairs anyway."

Gammon knocked on Cook's door.

John Gammon Peak District Detective

"Morning Amanda."

"Yes, morning John pull up a chair."

"This sounds all official?"

"Not really, I just know you won't be too pleased with what I have to say."

"Fire away Amanda."

"Clive Wiggledon won't be prosecuted by Bixton police."

"What?"

"I have just had the head of MI5 on to say because of the seriousness of his crimes it is of national importance that they have been given the task of extracting everything. Then they will decide what to do. He could become a major snitch for the intelligence people John."

"Do you know Amanda this job stinks, his last crime was on our patch."

THE SORROW BEGINS

"John at the end of the day your frustration is noted, and if it's any consolation I feel the same. He was our collar, but for the security of the country we have to put aside our personal gain."

"Look I don't want to get into an argument Amanda, but this is the second time this month. Imagine how I feel not just professionally but personally when a scum bag like Brian Lund is allowed back onto the streets of Derby. He causes pain and mayhem on anything he touches, and I am told they faked his death but now he is of use to them again. This man caused the break up and death of my family as well as numerous other families."

"John, I am truly sorry for you but Lund is off limits for us. If we attempt any connection or charges we will both be booted off the force."

"Well Amanda I am not sure I want to be on the force with these clowns running it. I best get the team together and tell them about Wiggledon and Lund. I'm sure that will go down like a lead balloon Amanda."

Cook just looked at Gammon. She knew he was right but her hands were tied.

Gammon got the team together in his office and gave them the grim news. At first the team were more concerned about Gammon with Lund actually alive and back in play. It wasn't long until it sunk in that all their hard work on Lund and Wiggledon seemed to be a waste of time. Gammon now took up the role that Amanda Cook had with him a few minutes early. After

THE SORROW BEGINS

five minutes they weren't happy, but he had got through to them about the greater good, so they left ok.

DI Milton stayed behind.

"Can I have a word John?"

"Of course Carl, how can I help you?"

"Look I don't want you to think I am some kind of nut case, but you said you might be able to pull some strings about Beth."

"I did Carl, my contact hasn't got back to me but as soon as they do I will let you know."

"Appreciate that John."

"Don't get your hopes up too high Carl."

"I won't," and Milton left the office.

Gammon knew it was a matter of Fleur contacting him and he had some serious questions to ask her. None more so than why she had lied about Brian Lund to him, knowing what it all meant. He could not let Lund take over his life again, the man was like a cat with nine lives. John decided he had to concentrate on the important things in life. He had his marriage to Saron and Christmas was coming. Hopefully Fleur would be in touch soon, there was no way Lund was going to affect that. John had one massive decision. He needed the operation to sort out the lodged bullet, but he decided he was getting married first. Then they could both make the decision. If the operation was to go wrong it would be something they both had to take.

THE SORROW BEGINS

There was a loud knock on Gammon's door. DCI Cook marched in.

"You ok Amanda?"

"Yes fine John, but not sure you will be?"

"Why what's a matter?"

"The Home Office wants you in London tomorrow."

"Whatever for?"

"I think they want to tell you about Lund and Wiggledon."

"Why me?"

"Well in Lund's case that affected your life and I think Wiggledon is a side issue, but they want to explain."

"Well they better have a good story Amanda."

"Just go and listen John. I suggest you get down there now. Stop in a hotel, your

John Gammon Peak District Detective

meeting is at the Craigmoor Hotel on Parliament Street at 9.30am."

"Who will be there?"

"They didn't say John, just go and listen."

Amanda turned to leave the office but before she disappeared to her office she turned around.

"John, we both know you should be a DCI, so don't let yourself down please," and she smiled.

John Gammon knew Amanda Cook was looking out for him. He left work at 4.00pm, nipped home and got an overnight bag from the cottage and headed for London. John knew the capital like the back of his hand and decided to book into the Craigmoor Hotel on Parliament Street. He

THE SORROW BEGINS

thought this would be less hassle in the morning.

The hotel was very plush, big chandeliers adorned every ceiling, the place oozed money. John got to his room, 309 on the third floor. Once inside the opulence was even grander. The bathroom was a full blown wet room. He had a double bed, a 60 inch curved screen TV and a small oak writing desk. Knowing the capital like the back of his hand he arranged a taxi to take him to Leicester Square and a little pub that he and Lindsay used to frequent. The Merlin was a pub just off the main area, so was generally filled with locals and a lot of Irish for some reason. John arranged for the taxi to pick him up at 11.30pm.

John Gammon Peak District Detective

John walked into the pub which was a real throw-back to the forties type pubs that adorned London during the war.

John knew what he was going to eat; the one and only Merlin cottage pie with chips and vegetables. He didn't know the guy behind the bar, but it had been a few years he thought. It was only 8.00pm so he found a seat in the window and waited in anticipation for his cottage pie. The chef always put juice from cranberries into the mash, then added double Gloucester on top. John wasn't disappointed when it arrived with broccoli and carrots.

The pub started to fill up and John was almost finished when he heard a call.

THE SORROW BEGINS

"Bloody John Gammon, as I live and breathe."

John turned to see a large man with a tweed jacket, corduroy trousers and brown brogues.

"Bloody hell, Billy Toad."

Billy Toad was a name given to Billy Warwick, to do with the way he dressed. They said he looked like a toad in a dinner suit.

"Here let me get you a drink, still Brandy and port mate?"

"Why not, only thing you can drink down here with your beer being like dishwater," and John laughed. Billy came back with the drinks.

"I thought you were living up North these days John?"

John Gammon Peak District Detective

"Yes, I am mate, work in a place called Bixton."

"Is that the place where the spring water comes from?"

"Certainly is Billy."

"How did Lindsay settle? Not seen her in years."

"We split mate and I am afraid she has passed away."

"Oh, I am sorry mate."

"New love on the horizon then John?"

"Yes mate, met a lovely girl and we are to be married Christmas Day."

"Well congratulations old boy."

"So, what about you Billy?"

"Still have a couple of antique shops in Camden and a couple in Covent Garden especially for the tourists. Also invested in

THE SORROW BEGINS

a good friend's internet business. Well when I say good friend, it was actually his son. He came up with the idea of selling chocolates and tinned stuff, you know mushy peas etc. abroad for ex pats. I only did it to help to be honest, and it took off. I invested a hundred grand and that gave me forty nine percent of the business. Well it took off all over the world. The business is turning over almost two million a year and growing. So, a good turn paid off John."

"Still come here then mate?"

"Yes, about twice a week. Rod Lester might be in soon. Remember Rod?"

"I remember smacking him one New Year's Eve for getting fruity with Lindsay, but looking back she was possibly egging him on."

John Gammon Peak District Detective

They carried on drinking and Rod Lester came in at 10.00pm. John and Rod shook hands and agreed the past was the past. At 11.00pm Rod said they should go to the Parrot Casino.

"Look lads I would love to, but got a mega meeting in the morning, so you two get off. My taxi is picking me up at 11.30pm. Rod and Billy exchanged numbers and promised to keep in touch. John finished his drink and true to his words the taxi driver was waiting as John stepped outside.

John knew he had more alcohol than he should have had but he had enjoyed seeing Billy after all these years.

THE SORROW BEGINS

Once back in the hotel John had a reasonable sleep and was awake at 8.00am. He showered and shaved, making sure his dark blue Paul Smith suit was perfect, and his cream shirt and tie was looking good. John made himself a coffee in the room and ate a small pack of Grimshaw's lavender and fruit biscuits. John wasn't a nervous person but he was feeling apprehensive about the meeting. John arrived in The Constable room, a beautiful oak paneled room with an enormous chandelier hanging from the ceiling which appeared to be the trend throughout the hotel.

Already in the room were Lady Dukerist, Police Complaints Director, Sir Andrew Wigg, Scotland Yard, Arthur Maine, MP in charge of overseeing police departments throughout the country. John sat down shaking hands with everyone as they had introduced themselves.

"Thank you for coming to the meeting today Mr Gammon. We have questions and explanations for you."

"Sir Andrew would you like to start."

"Thank you Lady Dukerist. DI Gammon, may we call you John?"

"Yes, that's fine."

"Ok John thank you. I would like to ask you about your career."

"In what respect?"

"Well I will be totally honest with you. You are a DI in a back-water county. When you were in London you were very highly thought of John."

THE SORROW BEGINS

"Well with the greatest of respect, I did make DCI, but because somebody on high didn't like my methods I was demoted."

"How do you feel about that John?"

"At the time it hurt, but I carry on doing my job and hopefully the rewards will follow."

"John, Arthur Maine, I have closely followed your career and have to say I didn't think you would have stayed at Derbyshire. I know you and your family is a Derbyshire family, but I do feel you are wasted in your current role. How do your family feel about this?"

John could not believe the stupidity of the man. Lady Dukerist did her best to resurrect the situation.

"I am assuming you have not been fully briefed. John lost his brother and mother in very sad circumstances and also his father, Arthur."

"Oh, I am sorry John, please accept my sincere condolences."

John nodded, what a prat he thought.

"Please don't think I am being forward, but where is all this leading?"

"Hi John, Andrew Wigg, I think we met a good few years ago."

"Yes, I think we did Sir Andrew, I believe it was a Christmas bash."

"Well John we called this meeting basically for me to measure if you still had the potential and the ambition. I think you do. The government are setting up a separate black ops division to tackle drugs. This will involve fifteen officers. In my opinion for it to be a success it will need a

THE SORROW BEGINS

man respected in the force that has a level head and lives the job. That's where you come in. It will be a DCI position with an excellent salary. The position is based in London but there will be a lot of travel initially. The new DCI will pick his own staff. Each member will be the man or woman he thinks can do the job."

"So why are you telling me this?"

"Because John we believe you are that man."

John was a bit stunned, he hadn't expected this.

"We don't expect an answer now. I suggest you take a couple of weeks and if you are interested then you can meet with me again, and we can discuss details. Does that sound fair John?"

John Gammon Peak District Detective

John was a little stunned. He thanked everyone, and said he would need the two weeks to think about it as he was getting married at Christmas.

They all shook hands and John went back to his room to get his bag and check out. He was feeling a little shocked at the offer.

John handed in his room key at reception and went to pay his bill. The young man on reception said it had been taken care of. John looked at his watch. It was now 3.30pm and he knew with traffic he could be back by 6.15pm. As he set off it was all sinking in. What a decision, this was a dream job for him.

THE SORROW BEGINS

The traffic was quite heavy, and it was almost 7.00pm as John came through Swinster. He knew he should go and see Saron to discuss what to do, but as always when he felt under pressure. Instead he went to Kev at the Spinning Jenny. John advanced down the worn stone steps to the main bar. Kev was sitting in the corner in his usual attire; white shirt, red dickie bow with his nose in The Racing Post.

"Evening lad, how are you?"

Kev's dulcet tones always made John feel comfortable.

"Hey Kev, I'm good, how are you?"

"Always good lad, what can I get you?"

"I'll have a pint of Pedigree mate please."

Kev returned with the Pedigree.

John Gammon Peak District Detective

"Quiet tonight mate."

"Yes, people stay in this time of year John, with Christmas around the corner. Not long to your big day lad."

"That's just it Kev. I need to speak to you."

"Not having second thoughts are you?"

"No Kev, just I have been to a meeting in London and been offered a great job."

"So, what's the problem?"

"Well this job is a complete blank canvas. I get the promotion to DCI. I choose all the officers, fifteen in total."

"So, what's the problem?"

"I would be based in London generally, but quite a lot of travel also. Saron is settled with the pub and now her mum is on her

THE SORROW BEGINS

own at Trissington Hall. I am sure she wouldn't move Kev."

"Have you spoke to her yet?"

"No mate came straight here. You know I appreciate your advice."

"I can see your dilemma mate. I know when we left Yorkshire after I took redundancy from the mine it was difficult to pull Doreen from her roots, and she did find it hard at first mate."

"What did I find hard?" came a voice from the hall leading to the kitchen.

"Nothing my love, just telling John that you found it a bit difficult leaving Yorkshire."

"Oh, and you didn't? I remember every Saturday when Wednesday were at home and you couldn't go because of the pub. You were always in a strop."

John Gammon Peak District Detective

"Yes, I agree I missed my mates but we did alright, didn't we?"

"I don't have time for reminiscing. I have sixteen steak and onion pies needing my attention," and Doreen spun round and headed back to the kitchen.

"Well you two are helpful mate," and John laughed.

"When do you have to give a decision John?"

"They are letting me have two weeks mate."

"Well I am here, if you need to talk again. I'm going out in ten minutes mate. Off to the Licensees' Christmas Meeting in Micklock. Anouska is doing the bar tonight. Speak of the devil."

THE SORROW BEGINS

Anouska took her coat off to reveal a white see through blouse. She had a short tartan kilt on with dark tights and some black high heels. Certainly a different fashion than you would normally see in the Peak District.

"How are you John?" Anouska asked.

"I'm good thanks, how was your day with Carl?"

Anouska smiled at first then opened up a little.

"We had a nice day, well until we met Carl's mum and I am sure she didn't like me."

"I don't think it would be that Anouska. She is always funny with anybody who is out with Carl."

"Are you seeing each other again?"

John Gammon Peak District Detective

"I don't know, he never said and besides I am busy here at the Spinning Jenny most nights."

The bar filled but not with many people John knew. So, at 10.30pm he left.

The ride down to the cottage was quite enchanting. He saw a stag, a badger and a big dog fox as he approached his cottage.

John's cleaner had been in that morning and the house was immaculate. He loved it when Phyllis Swan came to clean, it always had that fresh smell about it. John poured himself a Jameson's, put his Rab quilted coat on and sat in the garden. It was a fresh night but one of those where you feel great to be alive. John sat thinking about the future. The job he had been offered was tailor made for him. He felt excited inside

THE SORROW BEGINS

but then reality was how could he persuade Saron to leave the Peak District? Saron was settled, she had the pub business and was close to her mum. For John it was relatively easy, no family, just friends left in the Peak District now. Before he knew it he had consumed half the bottle of Jameson's. It had now turned quite nippy so he made his way to bed.

John Gammon Peak District Detective

CHAPTER NINE

Gammon arrived at Bixton police station at 8.50am.

"Morning Sergeant Yap."

"Good morning Sir."

"Is DCI Cook in?"

"No Sir, she won't be in until this afternoon apparently."

"Ok, anything to tell me?"

"No Sir, all quiet on the western front."

"Ok Ian, paperwork it is then."

"Sooner you than me Sir." Gammon grabbed a coffee and headed for his office.

Gammon was quite pleased with his progress with the paperwork and reports he had got through so he stopped for another coffee. As he stepped out of office Sergeant

THE SORROW BEGINS

Yap was on his way to his office, so they met at the door.

"Sir, another body has been found."

"Where Sergeant?"

"Well it's a bit weird. He has been found at what was Sterndales farm at Lingcliffe. Now being built on and called Une Vie Paisible. Don't know what it means Sir."

"Peaceful Life Sergeant, but not it seems for our victim Sergeant Yap."

"Forensics are on their way. I radioed DI Smarty and DI Scooper and they are heading there."

"Ok grab DI Milton, he can come with me."

Gammon nipped back to the office and grabbed his coat, meeting Milton in the car park. They headed to the development in Lingcliffe.

Gammon and Milton arrived. It wasn't the best of days, very wet and windy. Gammon could see the white tent had been set up by John Walvin's forensic team, and Smarty and Scooper had taped off the incident area.

"What we got Dave?"

"It's believed to be Alec Blake. The General Manager of the site found the body at the back of his cabin this morning."

Gammon put his head in the tent.

"Time of death Wally?"

"Bloody hell John, I'm not Harry Potter."

"I think you are mate."

THE SORROW BEGINS

"I would say sometime between 4.00am to 6.00am this morning. Other than that you will have to wait until the morning."

"Have we had a definite identification DI Smarty?"

"Well the General Manager said it's Alec Blake."

"Where is he?"

"He is in his cabin."

"Ok DI Milton, come with me. Let's talk to this guy."

The bright yellow work cabin stuck out like a sore thumb. Gammon knocked on the door and entered.

"DI Gammon and DI Milton, we believe you found the body. Your name is?"

"Les Belton."

John Gammon Peak District Detective

"Mr Belton, just run over the circumstances you found yourself in this morning."

"Well I arrived at 8.00am as I always do. I put the kettle on. We were having a big delivery of concrete at 9.30am. so I planned on a quick drink. Then I was going onto the site to speak with the men. Anyway, with the weather being so bad I needed a leak and to walk over to the thunder box."

"Thunder box Sir?"

"Sorry, we call the toilets the thunder box Mr Gammon."

"Ok carry on."

"Well I thought I would nip round the back of cabin and that's when I found Mr Blake."

THE SORROW BEGINS

"How well did you know Mr Blake?"

"Well he was one of the gaffers, you know, from the consortium."

"How well did you get on with Mr Blake?"

Les Belton was quite a big man with a leather jacket and a black moustache, and quite a chain smoker.

"I would be lying if I said he was my favourite person, but he had money tied up in this project, and I suppose that in itself is pressure."

"So are you saying you argued?"

"No, Mr Blake wasn't a man that would argue. He had his own way of getting back at you."

"Can you explain?"

"Look Mr Gammon, I need to get down on site."

John Gammon Peak District Detective

"Ok Mr Belton, I may need to call you in for questioning sometime soon."

"Not a problem Mr Gammon, now if you don't mind," and Belton brushed past Gammon.

Gammon thought how much his breath smelt of tobacco and possibly whisky as he brushed past him.

"Come on Carl, get Dave and Sandra and let's get back to the station. Tell Sandra I want her looking into Blake's finances. You and Smarty look into his past history, lets see if he had any skeletons. I will go and see Mrs Blake to let her know of her husband's demise."

"Ok John see you at the station later. I'll get a lift back with Dave and Sandra."

THE SORROW BEGINS

John doubled checked with Wally to be sure he would have something by 9.00am. He said that should be fine, so Gammon set off to see Mrs Blake.

Blake had lived in Ackbourne, number 14 Kempton Mews, a select six house development on the outskirts of the town. All the houses were six bedroomed with three en-suite, very exclusive houses.

Gammon pulled up at the house and parked in front of the double garage. There was a new Porsche which he assumed was Mrs Blake's. Gammon rang the doorbell which chimed to the sound of Love Me Tender. After a few seconds an attractive woman in her mid forties answered the door.

"Can I help you?"

John Gammon Peak District Detective

Gammon showed her his warrant card.

"Mrs Blake?"

"Yes," she replied.

"May I come in?"

"Yes, what is this about?"

"Do you have anybody that could come over?"

"No, why?"

"Please take a seat Mrs Blake."

"Well actually Alec and me have been together fifteen years, but we haven't got married. Please call me Sarah."

"Sarah, I am very sorry to say your partner was found dead this morning."

"What do you mean?"

"Alec is in Somerset on business."

Gammon was now concerned that the body wasn't Alec Blake and that they had

THE SORROW BEGINS

got it wrong. Luckily Gammon could see a picture of Alec on the sideboard, and unless he had a perfect double, the body Gammon saw this morning was certainly Alec Blake.

Sarah seemed calm but upset.

"Ok Sarah, I can arrange for a police liaison officer to stay with you. I would request you come to the station tomorrow to identify the body, Sarah."

"If you could arrange for the liaison officer please."

"Do you have children together?"

"No, Alec was married before and had three children, but none of them would speak to him. You see he left their mother for me."

"Did they get divorced?"

"Yes they did, Mr Gammon."

John Gammon Peak District Detective

The liaison officer arrived which allowed John to leave. Sarah said she would identify the body at 10.00am in the morning. Gammon headed back to Bixton but noticed he had a missed call. He tried to ring the number but it said he was blocked. There was a message though which Gammon pulled over to listen to.

"John, hi it's Fleur. I haven't got a lot of time but I will hopefully be at your wedding. Oh, and take the job, it's made for you," and Fleur hung up.

It suddenly dawned on Gammon that maybe his sister was behind the job offer. Oh, how he wished he could talk to her right now. Gammon pulled into Bixton at the same time as DCI Cook.

THE SORROW BEGINS

"Get in John, let's have a coffee in town."

Amanda took them to the Lavender Experience, a neat coffee shop in the centre of Bixton. John ordered two coffees and two Danish pastries. It was clear Amanda had been filled in with regard to John's meeting in London.

"So mystery man, what are you going to do?"

"I honestly don't know. If the offer had come five month ago I think I would have jumped at it. I mean who wouldn't the job is so me."

"Well on a personal note, I would hate to lose you as a friend. I would not blame you, as you say who wouldn't like that opportunity?"

John Gammon Peak District Detective

John knew he couldn't mention about Fleur. Talking to Amanda he began to wonder with the past events regarding Lund and Wiggledon maybe they wanted him out of the way? What better way than to move him to London and set up the new division, which could take three years to organise. John asked Amanda to be honest with him.

"John, you are being paranoid. You are a great officer and this is a fair reward for what you have done. What does Saron think?"

"I haven't told her yet."

"Why John?"

"Well I was late back last night. Oh, let me be honest, I would like this job but I can't see Saron leaving her life, and I am betrothed to her, Amanda."

THE SORROW BEGINS

"Well as my old dad would have said 'Everything comes to he who waits'."

"We shall see Amanda. Come on we best get back."

Amanda and John arrived back at Bixton station at 4.10pm. Gammon told DCI Cook he wanted to clear his paperwork, then was going to the Tow'd Man to speak with Saron

By 6.00pm Gammon had completed what he needed to do, and arranged for Sergeant Yap to ensure the team were in the incident room for 9.00am the following morning.

"Do you want John Walvin in there as well Sir?"

"Of course, not much good without his report on Alec Blake."

John Gammon Peak District Detective

"Ok Sir, see you tomorrow. Oh, Sir be careful it's been snowing quite heavy for an hour now."

"Ok thanks Sergeant Yap."

Gammon went out to the car park. There was already an inch of snow, he estimated, covering the car park. When it snowed in the Peak District Bixton was always the first to get it.

John arrived at the Tow'd Man where the car park was empty. He knew there would not be many people out tonight. John headed for the kitchen. Saron was prepping vegetables.

"Hello lovely. Where have you been?"

"Look let me makes us a coffee, we need to talk."

THE SORROW BEGINS

"That's sounds ominous, John Gammon!"

"No, not really, come and sit over here."

John made two coffees and sat across from Saron.

"A couple of days ago DCI Cook told me I had been invited to a meeting in London. She or I hadn't got a clue what it was about."

"So, what was it about?"

"I met four big hitters. They sat me down and offered me a new position as a DCI over a totally new division. I would have fifteen hand- picked officers, all of which I would pick."

"Sounds great John."

John Gammon Peak District Detective

"Well that's the good bit. The bad bits are, I'm sorry we would be based in London with me doing a lot of travelling."

Saron's head went down.

"When do you have to tell them?"

"I have two weeks sweetheart."

Saron didn't say anymore other than she had to crack on with the vegetables. As she got up John held her arms.

"It would be for us Saron, not just me."

She smiled, "I know John just let it sink in please."

"Shall I stay tonight Saron?"

"No, you get off go and have a drink with Kev. I will be busy doing this until midnight and won't be much company."

John kissed her and left. As he was driving down to the Spinning Jenny he

THE SORROW BEGINS

thought to himself, well that went down like a lead balloon.

Luckily it had stopped snowing and the drive to the Spinning Jenny was magical with the trees overhanging with snow, and the roads glistening on the approach to Swinster.

The pub car park was full, and he wandered down the stone steps from the car-park into the pub. The pub was quite busy seeing the weather had been so bad early on. John realised it was the Hittington WI pre-Christmas bash. The first person he bumped into was Sheba Filey.

"Hey, hello lover boy."

John smiled.

"Pleased you have come, you can have a book of raffle tickets off me."

John Gammon Peak District Detective

John handed over five pounds. Sheba gave John her usual foxy look as she carried on going around the pub selling the tickets. John advanced to the bar. It was good to see Cheryl, Bob, Jack and Shelley.

"No Carol tonight?"

"She is in the States with her mum, John."

Cheryl leaned forward and whispered in John's ear.

"You are a good man John Gammon. That was so kind what you have done for Freda Lestar."

"Have you met Jill and Kevin Antliff? They have moved into Swinster, both retired so living the good life. This is the famous John Gammon."

THE SORROW BEGINS

"Oh wow, you are the guy that catches all these killers. I have seen you on the telly."

"Not just me Jill, we are a team at Bixton."

"So where are you two from?"

"Well Kev is from the Isle of Man originally, but he was in the Navy for years. I was born in Ackbourne but we moved away when I was eight. I was a friend of Cheryl's at junior school, and we sort of kept in touch. I ended up in Gloucester working at a nuclear research facility for many years. With us both having good jobs we decided, on a whim to be honest, to come back here. I saw the Hobbit Cottage in Swinster, and I remembered a friend of mine and Cheryl's, Myra Michaels lived there. Anyway we came up and bought it there and then. I think it had been sold twice more after I left, so don't know what happened to Myra.

"I know the cottage Jill, it's quite big down a drive, isn't it?"

"Yes, with Wisteria all over the front façade. It really is lovely, John."

"Yes, remember it Cheryl."

"Here Bob got you a Pedigree."

"Cheers mate."

"So, what's it like to be back Jill?"

"It's only been a week; poor Kev feels like he is in a whirlwind with me showing him round. Had a nice meal at the Sycamore at Pritwich with Bob and Cheryl last night. I just love these little pubs."

"You got children Kev?"

THE SORROW BEGINS

"Yeah, Rod he lives in Gloucester and Sally she lives in Manchester."

"Well you aren't too far from either of them mate."

"You know kids John, bank of dad and all that," and Kev laughed.

"Well, I'm sure you will enjoy our social circle mate. Listen, I'm not being rude, just need a quick word with Kev."

"No problem John, great to meet you mate."

John wandered over to the bar. Kev had Tracey Rodgers, Anouska, Joni and himself behind the bar.

"Hello lad, thought you weren't talking."

"Sorry Kev, just met Cheryl and Bob's friends."

"Seem like nice people John."

"Yeah, think they will fit in mate. Have you spoke with Saron?"

"Yes, mate tonight."

"Oh, so that's why you are here then. I take it didn't go down to well?"

"Something like that. Well I guess it's a big shock it would totally change her life. I really don't know what to do Kev."

"Give her some space mate. I am sure you two will sort it out one way or the other."

Kev wandered off to serve some more people. John ordered a round of drinks for Bob, Cheryl and everyone in the group, which now included Sheba. He wandered back to the group.

"Time for the raffle results. I sold them Shelley, you announce them, ok."

THE SORROW BEGINS

"Ladies and Gentlemen, it's that time so here is a list of the prizes. First prize is a fifty five inch curved plasma smart TV. The second prize is a weekend for two in York. Third prize a meal here, kindly given by Kevin and Doreen. Fourth prize is a Chinese take away meal for four delivered to your house. The fifth and final prize is a bottle of ten year old whisky, kindly given by the Saron at the Tow'd man."

"Ok, first ticket is pink number 117."

Nobody shouted up so they looked at the address.

"It's Olivia Noon from Ackbourne."

"Ok second prize, it's a green ticket 301."

Nobody called again. Then Sheba realised she hadn't given John his tickets. He had won.

John Gammon Peak District Detective

"Jammy buggar John."

"Thanks Bob," and he laughed.

"Third prize, green ticket again 404."

A lady at the back came forward to claim her prize. The two final prizes were taken in the pub.

"So, John you win again?"

John laughed at the thought. He had won despite the situation with the job and Saron.

"What do you think Sheba?"

"Let's go over here John."

Sheba took John to the side room that wasn't as busy.

"You are not yourself John. Are you having second thoughts?"

THE SORROW BEGINS

John got them both a double brandy, and he started to unravel the situation to Sheba.

Sheba listened intensely as John told her about the job opportunity and the situation with Saron. Sheba took John's hand and led him outside. She held John close.

"I understand your dilemma John."

This was the first time Sheba had really shown her feelings to John.

"Look this isn't right, I am going inside Sheba."

Sheba smiled and followed John back into the busy bar. It was 10.40pm, so John slipped away. The last thing he needed was more complications.

John Gammon Peak District Detective

Gammon arrived at Bixton station the following morning hoping Wally had some good news for the 9.00am meeting.

Gammon went straight to the incident room. The room was full, they were waiting on Gammon and DCI Cook. Amanda Cook followed Gammon in. Gammon stood at the front.

"Ok everybody, as you are aware Alec Blake was found dead at Lingcliffe yesterday. I am troubled we have yet to get any concrete suspects, so I want to run through things after Wally has filled us all in on Alec Blake. Wally please."

John Walvin came to the front.

"Ok everybody, the body found yesterday believed to be Alec Blake of Ackbourne, but as yet not confirmed, as I

THE SORROW BEGINS

believe his partner is coming in this morning to identify the body. Right, we found like with the other two bodies, that this man had what looked like whip marks on his back and buttock consistent I believe with some kind of sexual act. This man had also been strangled. The strange thing was I could not see that he put up a struggle. This led me to think that he may have been drugged. We checked him for alcohol and he was three times over the legal limit. We then checked for drugs we found traces of cocaine and Rohypnol Flunitrazepan, commonly known as a date rape drug. This man was rendered useless, hence no struggle."

"So, do we all think this was a murder or an accident? There was no wallet found

John Gammon Peak District Detective

on Mr Blake, therefore whoever did this must have it."

"DI Scooper, I want you to get an in-depth report on Blake's bank account."

"Ok thanks Wally, good job yet again."

"Ok this what we have.
Victim One: Duncan Mule, I won't go through the injuries because they all have the same and they have all been strangled.
Victim Two: Roger Thorndyke
Victim Three: Alec Blake.
I'll throw this out to you. We all know the suspects, they are part of this consortium. Who thinks Robinson Spencer could be our murderer and why?"

"Yes," DI Milton.

"Spencer isn't a nice guy, he already has form having been to prison for

THE SORROW BEGINS

attacking Pamela Mule and trying to burn their house down."

"Do you not feel he did that when he was younger, and maybe he has learnt his lesson, DI Milton?"

"Possibly Ma'am, but once a bad un always a bad un, we say round here."

"Yes, DI Scooper."

"Personally I think it could be Rod Goff that killed Mule because of his daughter. I know how I would feel with Rosie, Ma'am."

"But what about the other two?"

"Maybe there are two killers Ma'am?"

"Ok thank you Sandra."

"DI Smarty, oh and Sergeant Magic?"

"For certain we both think Phil Sterndale. He has the motive and the physical attributes to carry these murders out."

"John what are your thoughts?"

"I am quite open to be honest, but I do feel there is some underlying association with Maggie Silito, Ma'am."

"Well it appears we all have a different view, which isn't always bad. Well go on then, ask me who I think our murderer is?"

They all laughed, Amanda Cook had a good way of keeping close to the team.

"I think Philip Sterndale stands out, but I don't think it's quite as cut and dry as that. The woman he is seeing, do we have any information on her?"

This was a glaring miss by the team and John felt quite embarrassed.

THE SORROW BEGINS

"Ok well John, bring her in, and she needs a solicitor as well. I would like to be in the interview when you do it."

"Yes Ma'am."

"Ok thanks everybody, let's keep digging."

As they were leaving Carl grabbed John.

"Any news John?"

"Sorry mate, they haven't been in touch."

John could feel Carl's disappointment but unless he could speak to Fleur, which was almost impossible, he doubted he could help Carl.

Gammon arranged for Yap to get Sterndale's girlfriend in and to be sure she brought a solicitor. It was just after lunch when Sergeant Yap let John know that

John Gammon Peak District Detective

Annie Frokel would be at the station by 3.00pm, so John let DCI Cook know.

Annie Frokel arrived with her solicitor and a very agitated Phil Sterndale. Gammon and Cook went down and could hear the commotion as they headed for the front desk.

"Oh Gammon, what the hell as this got to do with Annie?"

"We don't rule out anybody, Mr Sterndale."

"You are bloody nuts, those three all deserved to die. I take my hat off to whoever did it."

"Be careful, Mr Sterndale."

THE SORROW BEGINS

Gammon gestured to Frokel and her solicitor as he headed to interview room one.

The tape was set by Sergeant Magic. Present were Annie Frokel, her solicitor, a Derek Tyde, DCI Gammon and DCI Cook.

"Miss Frokel, may we call you Annie?"

"Yes, that will be fine," she replied.

"What country are you from?"

"Poland."

"Nice accent," Gammon said to the curly ginger haired woman.

"Why is my client here Mr Gammon?"

"Well Mr Tyde, we currently have three unsolved murders in the Peak District. One of the suspects is Philip Sterndale and we believe your client is in a relationship with Mr Sterndale."

"Is that correct Annie?"

John Gammon Peak District Detective

"Yes, I see Philip."

"So, you would know about the hatred Philip has towards the so-called syndicate?"

"I would Mr Gammon, they are very evil men only interested in profit and themselves."

"Elaborate then Annie."

"The syndicate took everything that Philp's family had, even their self-respect."

"So, you and Philip decided to kill these evil men, as you put it Annie."

Annie laughed out loud, flicking her long red curly hair. She smiled at her solicitor.

"I must say Miss Frokel, I find your contempt for this interview a little disturbing."

Gammon butted in.

THE SORROW BEGINS

"Why did you leave Poland?"

"Promise of a better life in England."

"How long have you been here?"

"Three and a half years."

"What is your job?"

"How can I put this? I am what you would call a pleasure dome mistress."

"What exactly is a pleasure dome mistress?"

"I give pleasure to gentlemen."

"So, you prostitute yourself for money then Annie?"

"Oh, please put away the age old adage, it's a little tiresome."

"So where is the pleasure dome Annie?"

"Why, would you like an appointment Mr Gammon? I think I would not charge you with being so handsome?"

John Gammon Peak District Detective

"Sadly I wasn't asking for me Annie, purely part of the investigation."

"Well I am sorry, I don't have to tell you where I operate."

"No, you don't but if you are involved in any way with these victims, or are holding back on any information then you could be liable for a long prison sentence."

Again Annie laughed; it was if she was being protected in some way.

"So, Annie, are you telling us you have no knowledge of the murders?"

"Mr Gammon you bring me here today in a very hostile manner, but we Polish people are not easily intimidated. Now if you are finished with me I will be on my way."

THE SORROW BEGINS

Gammon looked at DCI Cook. She nodded.

"Interview ended, the time is 4.58pm 2nd December."

"Thank you Mr Gammon," the solicitor said as he ushered his client out of the room.

"Well Ma'am, I don't know what we got from that?"

"I think we got a lot, look at it from a different angle John. We have three people dead who appeared to have been involved in some kind of sexual gratification, and Annie Frokel is clearly in that trade. I suggest we dig deep on this woman. Put an officer on her twenty four seven. Let's see where she plies her trade."

John Gammon Peak District Detective

CHAPTER TEN

John arranged the cover to watch Annie Frokel and got Milton looking into her finances etc.

It was time to go home and John decided to call Saron to see if the ice had broken. Saron seemed ok, so John said he would drop in. He left Bixton and headed for the Tow'd Man. As always the drive was breath-taking. John stuck to the backroads which still had the snow. He arrived at the pub at 6.20pm.

John went down the back steps knowing Saron would be in the kitchen. But the kitchen was in darkness so he carried onto the bar. Donna Fringe was behind the

THE SORROW BEGINS

bar and was very pleased to see John, so much so, she came from behind the bar and flung her arms round him.

"John, it is so lovely to see you. How are you and the team?"

"Yeah, we are good. You look so well Donna."

"Think it's because I am happy John, I love this business."

"I am pleased for you Donna."

Just then Saron came in the bar. She looked stunning in a white blouse and brown trousers.

"Hey John, I am having the night off, do you want to go out or stay here."

"I am ok here, if you are?"

"Ok, get that window seat and I'll bring some drinks over."

John Gammon Peak District Detective

John sat in the window thinking how well this was going.

As Saron walked towards him John was transfixed. She just oozes class he thought?

"You look lovely sweetheart."

"Thank you John. So have you thought anymore about the job?"

"Thought about it a lot Saron."

"Have you come up with a decision?"

"No way, we do this together."

"Are you sure John?"

"Of course I am sure Saron, we are to be man and wife."

"Well John I have thought about that, and it's not too late to change your mind. I won't hold it against you."

"What are you saying?"

THE SORROW BEGINS

"I am giving you a get out of jail free card."

"Saron, I intend marrying you. If that means I don't take the job so be it."

This was all music to her ears.

"Look John I have spent a few sleepless nights going over this. I have my business and my mum needs me close. I have everything, and if we are to get married as planned then my fairy tale is complete."

"Then let's forget it. I want what you want Saron."

"But you have to be sure John, otherwise this dream will collapse around us, don't you think?"

"I know what you are saying, and I truly want what you want. No job is worth losing you, so I will call them in the morning and decline it. I want one promise from you though."

"Anything John."

"Get some staff for the kitchen, so we can have some time together when we are married."

"Already thought of that John and I promise I will. Can I be excited about the wedding now?"

"Of course, you can."

"I have asked Jo to be chief bridesmaid. My nieces from Ireland who are fifteen and seventeen are the other two."

"Steve is the best man for me, and apparently we are going to Dublin next weekend, if you are ok with that?"

"Of course, you enjoy."

THE SORROW BEGINS

"So, are you pleased with your wedding dress?"

"Over the moon. Mum has arranged the big marquee plus three other marquees. We have a band on and a disco. The church is all sorted. I am just hoping for some snow John and I think it will be perfect."

John could see how much this meant to Saron and he wasn't going to ruin it. John knew he wanted to settle down and have a family. What better place in the world than the Peak District he thought?

"John, I know you don't want to go into detail too much, but what colour suit are you wearing, only the bridesmaids are wearing a darkish blue?"

"Funny that, I was going to wear my Paul Smith dark blue suit."

John Gammon Peak District Detective

"That will be perfect," she hugged John. "I am so happy."

It was 11.30pm and Saron locked up. Donna had gone to bed, she had been up early doing breakfast for the three guests they had in.

"Bed time John Gammon," she said as she held John's hand and led him upstairs.

"Get in bed John while I nip to the bathroom."

John almost nodded off, Saron must have been gone twenty minutes. John wasn't disappointed when Saron entered the bedroom. She was a classically beautiful woman. Her blonde hair cascaded over her porcelain coloured skin, over her shoulder and then down her back. Saron's figure was

THE SORROW BEGINS

as good as anything anyone would see. Her figure complemented the white basque she wore with white stockings, and a pair of kitten heel shoes trimmed with white fur. She simply looked stunning. John felt like a very lucky man.

Saron straddled John kissing him passionately first on the lips then working her way down his torso. Then love and lust took over and they made love, first Saron on top, then John until they both were satisfied with a wave of ecstasy and fulfiment.

"I love you John Gammon," she said as she lay playing with hairs on John's chest.

"I love you too my lovely. I'm sorry about the job."

"You have nothing to be sorry for John. I know your ambition and what your job means to you, but I do know our best chance is here in the Peak District."

"I know that now Saron. To be honest I think I knew that during the meeting in London, but sometimes ego takes over."

"Can we forget it now John and concentrate on our wedding?"

"Of course."

"So, John Gammon living in a pub, is that good?" she laughed.

"Sounds good to me."

The following morning Saron was up and cooked John a full English breakfast.

"Don't think you are getting this everyday Mr Gammon."

"Perhaps as well or I would be a Michelin man," and he laughed.

THE SORROW BEGINS

"Listen Saron, it's my stag do on Saturday you, ok with that?"

"Of course, I am. Got a busy weekend anyway, it's all starting for Christmas now."

"Great, well look sweetheart I best go back to mine tonight and get stuff ready for Saturday."

"Just don't get into any trouble, you know how Steve can get after a few beers."

"No problem, Bob and Jack will keep us in check."

John left and headed for the station and a meeting with DCI Cook to tell her his decision.

"Morning Sergeant Yap, is DCI Cook in yet?"

"In her office Sir."

John Gammon Peak District Detective

"Great thanks."

Gammon climbed the stairs and headed straight for Cook's office.

"Come in," she said answering the knock on her office door.

"Oh, good morning John, you ok?"

"Yes, fine Amanda."

"Come and take a seat."

"Well I was uncertain how to handle this with you being my commanding officer."

"Fire away John."

"I have decided not to take the job in London."

Gammon watched Amanda Cook's face and body language, she seemed relieved in some way.

THE SORROW BEGINS

"John for me personally I am so pleased. I have to ask you though, the job without doubt is a fantastic opportunity, I doubt if a job like that will ever come along again."

"I know Amanda, and yes it was everything I ever wanted. But Saron is above that and I can't lose her, I really can't Amanda."

"Would you like me to tell them John?"

"I don't want to break with protocol, so if that's ok with you."

"No problem John. Do you want to leave it until after lunch just to be sure?"

"No, my mind is made up but thank you."

John went to his office feeling like he had a great weight lifted off his shoulders.

John Gammon Peak District Detective

Gammon's desk was its usual overflowing state. He sat down and now that was done he needed to get his detective head on and get these murders cracked.

Gammon sat looking towards Losehill with a cup of coffee or dishwater as he called it. The view from his office window never ceased to amaze Gammon, and this time of the year was the best. He sat thinking about the honeymoon, knowing he could only have a couple of days away with the murder cases at such a high profile.

The weather looked bleak towards Losehill. It had a lot of snow on the top and looking at the sky even more to come. John felt strangely content when the phone rang. It was Sergeant Yap.

"I have a call for you Sir."

THE SORROW BEGINS

"Ok, thanks Sergeant."

"John?"

"Steve. Hi mate, sorry not been in touch it's been quite a week mate."

"No problem, just checking you are ok for Dublin tomorrow afternoon?"

"Yes, all good mate."

"Well listen, we all want a beer at the Spinning Jenny tonight can you make 7.00pm?"

"Yes mate, but no flippin' flabber-gram or anything daft, promise?"

"No, you are ok mate nothing daft. I promise."

"Right see you at 7.00pm. Are all the lads coming?"

"Oh yeah."

Steve rung off.

John Gammon Peak District Detective

John felt a bit apprehensive, but he sat at his desk and wrote down names of the murder victims, then the suspects.

Phil Sterndale had all the motives and now his girlfriend Annie Frokel was almost certainly involved in some way with the trade she was in. What is the connection he kept asking himself? All three men had visited somebody like Frokel or Maggie Silito. John realised these men were older, and maybe they went to these women on a regular basis. Ollie Watkins from the Old Court House in Swinster may be the next victim. It was almost 7.00pm so he decided to speak with Watkin on Monday.

Sergeant Yap and Di Trimble were changing over shifts, so John asked if Ian

THE SORROW BEGINS

Yap would like to come for a drink at the Spinning Jenny.

"That's very good of you Sir. I think DI Smarty invited John Walvin from Forensics."

"Ok mate, see you up there. Goodnight Di."

"Yes, goodnight Sir, have a nice weekend."

"Thanks Di."

John set off for the Spinning Jenny. It was a very cold night so the roads were icy and John knew he had to take his time down the back lanes.

Steve and the lads were at the Spinning Jenny. Kev had the night off which surprised John, with Doreen letting him go on the stag weekend to Dublin.

John Gammon Peak District Detective

"There you go mate," Steve said as he John entered the bar, and he handed him a Pedigree.

"Cheers mate."

"To our mate John Gammon," Steve said as he raised the toast.

They were a motley crew. Kev the landlord, Bob the comedian, Jack, Steve, Ian Yap, Dave Smarty, Carl Milton, David Magic and Peter Lee. Although Peter and Carl had volunteered to miss the stag do with everything going off at the station.

"Here you are lads."

Doreen appeared with sausage rolls, roast potatoes, pork pies and quiches.

"I am good to you lot, and didn't even get asked on the stag weekend."

She left planting a kiss on John's cheek.

THE SORROW BEGINS

"Have a great weekend love."

"Thanks Doreen," and she smiled as she headed for the kitchen.

"Wow Kev, this is excellent mate."

"Yeah, she is a good one, my Doreen is Steve."

"You can say that again mate."

"So mate, I never thought I would ever be on John Gammon's stag do."

"Why not Bob?"

"Well you have the pick, don't you?"

"Not sure on that mate."

"What do you reckon Jack?"

"Well it is Saron he is marrying you know."

"Got to agree with you on that."

"You wouldn't swap your Doreen?"

"No, Doreen is the best for me lad."

John Gammon Peak District Detective

Steve got a game of darts going between the lads. Of course everyone had to put a fiver in, and with Steve being really good at darts it was a forgone conclusion he would win. But he didn't bargain on DI Lee. Steve and Peter reached the final with Peter whipping Steve three nil to win the money.

"Hard luck Stevie boy."

"Bollocks Kev, I was set up."

They all started laughing.

"Think darts was your idea, my friend."

Bob was rolling about laughing.

It was 11.15pm when the men's wives started arriving to pick them up.

"Don't forget lads, mini bus leaves here at 1.00pm tomorrow for East Midlands

THE SORROW BEGINS

airport and the flight to Dublin. Don't forget your passports."

John got Doreen to drop him home and she said she would pick him up at 12.45pm the next day. John went inside knowing in a couple of weeks he would be living at the Tow'd Man and a totally different life ahead of him.

John was up at 8.30am, made himself a slice of toast and marmalade and a strong black coffee. Once finished he set about packing some clothes. Deep down he wasn't really bothered about going but Steve had been his best mate for years, and he didn't want to let him or the others down.

Doreen arrived spot on time and took John to the Spinning Jenny. All the lads were already on the mini bus as Doreen dropped him on the car park. They were all singing 'You are late, you are late, you are late'. John smiled as he got on board.

The flight was seamless, and they arrived at the hotel in Dublin that Steve had booked. It was a four star hotel in the centre of the city.

They all started booking in.

"Right lads, quick shower then out?"

"Shall we say 8.00pm then Steve, in reception?"

"Good for me lads."

They went off to get showered. John was quite pleased with his room. He was thinking Jo must have booked this, as Steve would have had them in a flea pit, not a nice place like this.

THE SORROW BEGINS

John dressed casually and headed downstairs. Bob and Jack were already down with David Magic and Dave Smarty.

"Who are we waiting for?"

"Steve, Wally and Kev."

They could hear Steve coming down the stairs singing Take That's 'Could it Be Magic'. He was flanked on both sides with Wally and Kev.

"Right lads, O'Malleys bar first stop."

O'Malleys was your typical Irish tourist pub packed with music belting out from the far side of the room.

"Eight pints of Guinness mate please."

You could see the lad behind the bar had to put up with the stag night tourists on a regular basis but he did his job in a professional manner. They all got their beer. Right lads down in one, last one to finish gets the next round. David Magic came last bemoaning they all had a start on him.

"Right lads, out the door turn right, next is the Galway Hooker. No it's not a knocking shop lads, it's the name of a boat," and Steve laughed.

Once in the Galway Hooker Magic ordered the Guinness making sure he wasn't last to down it in one. They all finished but it was deemed by the group that Kev was last. This went on for a further three pubs. It was now almost 11.45pm. Kev and Wally said they were going back, so they all decided to go back as Steve had arranged a trip round the Jameson distillery the following morning.

THE SORROW BEGINS

They arrived back, and Steve was reveling in being the organiser.

"Ok lad, if you can be in reception for 11.00am, that's when we get picked up."

"What time are they serving breakfast until Steve?"

"10.00am Magic."

"Brill, brekkie then off to the distillery."

"Oh, and straight after the distillery we are going horse racing so hope you've brought lots of money lads."

The distillery was right up everyone's street, but Kev did make a pig of himself and was ill in the toilet. The others had paced themselves. Steve said he had booked a table for them at the races. The first race was 1.45pm and they arrived with just

John Gammon Peak District Detective

enough time to put their bets on. They decided that they would just have one horse per race and each pick a race. John went first and chose, Metal Mickey. The lads all went to the outside area of the box to watch the race.

On the run it was between Metal Mickey and Saratoga Lady. Metal Mickey hit the final fence but rallied on the long run in to win by half a length. The lads all started singing, 'One John Gammon, there's only One John Gammon'. John gave Kev the ticket as he had stopped drinking and said he would put the bets on and collect any winnings.

"What price did we get Kev?"

"Eight to one Bob."

"Love it mate."

THE SORROW BEGINS

Kev had put twenty on from each member making a hundred and sixty pounds, at eight to one a total of twelve hundred and eighty pounds in total.

"Great start lads."

"Here we got you a gin and tonic Kev."

"Thanks lads, but not for me. I'll stick with the orange juice for now, overdid the whisky but thanks."

"Come on Bob, your pick."

"It has to be The Comedian."

"Nice one mate, it's joint second favourite."

The race started. Poor Bob, his pick came last. Bob felt bad and the lads made him feel worse, but that was all part of the banter. The next four races were all lost, but then it was Dave Smarty's pick.

John Gammon Peak District Detective

"Look lads, I have never picked a horse in my life. Let Kev do mine, he understands horses."

"No way Dave, this one is down to you."

"Ok Steve, as long as you know we are chucking the money away."

Dave chose Chocolate Drop. When Kev came back from putting it on he was laughing.

"Only bloody thirty three to one, Dave."

"Well I did warn everyone."

They went wild watching Chocolate Drop storm home and win by five lengths.

"Flippin' heck Kev how much will that make?"

THE SORROW BEGINS

"Five thousand two hundred and eighty pounds for us. Dave well done mate."

"I can't believe it."

"Right last race, who's turn is it?"

"Mine."

"Come on then Steve let's finish it off while we are well on top."

"Right, I fancy Knitting Yarn."

"Ok back in a minute," and Kev went off to put the money on the last pick.

"Only nine to four lads."

They all got a beer and stood watching. It was a close run race but sadly Knitting Yam could only make third.

"Right come on lads back to the hotel, it's beer night."

"He is bloody animal," Bob said to Jack.

John Gammon Peak District Detective

"Yeah, know what you mean, a cup of tea would do me mate."

"Me as well Jack."

Steve said everyone had to be down for 8.00pm. They would only be out until 1.00am as they had to be back at the airport for the flight back at 10.00am. They all gathered in reception as Steve instructed. Bob was a few minutes late having fallen asleep.

"Right lads, as the final surprise we are going to the VIP lounge at Mary Ann's Nightclub. This nightclub is famous it's where Bono, Geldof and all the top celebrities hang out."

John sat with Steve on the way to the club.

THE SORROW BEGINS

"Mate, I just want to say thanks for a great stag weekend."

"Yeah, winning that money on the horses was a flippin' bonus mate."

"No, everything it's been good."

"Well you have Jo to thank. To be honest I was going to get you a big flabbergram but she wouldn't let me."

"You have a lovely girl there, mate."

"Yeah, we have both been lucky John. Have to say though mate, never thought you would settle. I mean you have been a bit of lad of late, John."

"I know what you are saying mate, but I want what you have. I need to be settled."

"Glad to hear it John, really pleased for you."

They arrived at the club and it was a tribute night with four groups and a disco.

John Gammon Peak District Detective

T Rex, Slade, Who and Rod Stewart plus the disco. Kev was back on form and was soon up and dancing with some dark-haired woman, doing his best Mark Bolan impression. Bob decided to do his best John Travolta impersonation. The night was excellent although Steve did fall out with a couple of Irish lads, but John managed to calm it down. They arrived back at the hotel and everyone went to bed, but Steve insisted on buying John a last brandy in the hotel bar.

"Two large brandies please."

"I'm only having this, then I'm off to bed Steve."

"Ok mate, just thought it would be a nice end to your stag do."

THE SORROW BEGINS

"It is mate, sorry got work on my mind."

"Understand mate you, have had a rough couple of years."

"It's got worse Steve. The man that got my brother so upset, and that he thought he had killed, well he hadn't. This guy has more lives than a cat. He is back in Derby and there is nothing I can do about it. I turned down a job in London for Saron. Really, I would love to have taken it."

"So, you really are smitten with Saron then?"

By now they had almost half a bottle of brandy inside them.

"Look mate I'm off to bed."

"Ok John, and look mate I know with everything we don't see enough of each other, so we must try harder. I am always here for you mate, you know that."

"Love you Steve, you are the best."

"Goodnight mate, don't be late for the taxi to the airport."

John smiled and Steve carried on talking to the young barmaid.

The following morning they all assembled in the reception ready for the taxi to the airport. Steve came downstairs looking dreadful.

"Blimey mate, what time did you get to bed?"

"Twenty minutes ago."

They all laughed but John knew Steve was being truthful.

THE SORROW BEGINS

"I best get everyone organised then," said Kev.

"Well I would suggest you wipe that lipstick off your forehead mate or Doreen will bloody eat you alive."

"Oh crap, I didn't do anything only dance, Jack."

"I know Kev, no worries it was just a bit of fun."

"You know what they say Kev 'what happens in Dublin stays in Dublin'."

"Bollocks Bob."

They were all laughing.

On arrival at the airport the plane was on time. They all seemed cheerful except for poor Steve who just looked dreadful. It was 3.30pm when they arrived back at the Spinning Jenny.

"Are you all coming in for a drink?"

John Gammon Peak District Detective

Rapturous clapping followed Kev's suggestion.

"Oh, and Bob don't be saying anything silly please. You know Doreen."

"I won't mate."

John told Anouska that the drinks from now until the last person left were on his tab. With a beer in hand John wandered over to Kev.

"Been a good weekend mate."

"Yes, enjoyed it John.

"Had a bit too much whisky at the distillery, but other than that really had a good time, and the winnings at the races weren't half bad mate."

"No, I was chuffed with that Kev."

By 8.00pm everyone had been picked up. Jo was picking Steve up so John asked

THE SORROW BEGINS

for a lift home. Whilst he had enjoyed the weekend he was ready for his own bed, and he knew he had to start getting results in the murder cases.

John was up and dressed and in work for 8.30am. He was keen to spend some time in the incident room looking to see if he had missed anything. He told Sergeant Yap to get Annie Frokel in at 9.30am and Maggie Silito for 10.30am. John stood with a cup of coffee. Could he count any of the suspects out? He looked at Robison Spencer knowing Spencer had served time for his attack on Pamela Mule, and for trying to burn down their house. Whilst not good, John wrote on his writing pad 'not enough to make him number one suspect.' He then looked at Rod Goff and the altercation some years before with Duncan Mule. Gammon wrote 'no way, too many years before.' He then looked at Phil Sterndale. He wrote on his pad 'very possible, motive, hatred and Annie Frokel'. He then looked at Bobby Lint, 'motive greed' he wrote. 'Nose put out of joint, friends with all murdered, not allowed in on the consortium scheme, didn't like Thorndyke'. He sat with his coffee looking at his pad. Is that it he thought? At best two real suspects in his mind. Gammon felt hopeless, nothing was hitting him like other cases. His coffee was almost cold when Sergeant Yap came in to say Annie Frokel and her solicitor were here and in interview room one with DI Milton and DI Scooper.

"Thanks Ian, on my way."

THE SORROW BEGINS

Gammon turned over the front cover on his writing pad and headed to the interview. He sat across from Frokel, he was in no mood to play games.

"Ok Annie, I want answers from you. Our latest victim, Alec Blake, one of the consortium had the same markings on his back and most of his body that the other victims had. Did you or any of your staff inflict these?"

She simply said, "No comment."

"Do you make your living by inflicted these things on men?"

"No comment."

"How long have you done this type of work?"

"No comment."

"Annie Frokel, you are trying my patience."

John Gammon Peak District Detective

Annie Frokel just looked straight ahead. Gammon turned to Daniel Miles her solicitor.

"Mr Miles, you need to ensure your client is fully aware of her non-communication in these murder inquiries."

Daniel Miles stood up.

"If you are not going to charge my client with anything then this interview is over, DI Gammon."

Gammon was bursting inside. What an arrogant man, but he knew he had nothing yet again. He looked at Milton.

"Interview terminated."

Milton stopped the tape. He pushed his card at Annie Frokel.

"I know you have been got at, if you need to speak with me my number is there."

THE SORROW BEGINS

Frokel's piercing green eyes looked at Gammon one last time before she left.

With everyone out of the room. DI Scooper spoke with Gammon.

"We will get who is doing this John. I agree she had been got at, but we have never failed before."

"Come on Sandra, let's hear what Maggie Silito has to say."

Silito was in interview room one. Milton was again in charge of recording and Gammon and Scooper sat across from Maggie Silito who had refused a solicitor.

"Ok Maggie, are you sure you don't want any legal representation?"

She looked at Gammon and Scooper with a harsh look.

"NO."

John Gammon Peak District Detective

Gammon could sense a change in the persona of Maggie Silito. Whilst she wasn't the friendliest person he had ever met, she certainly wasn't this harsh person.

"Ok Maggie, we know you have people to your house, for shall we say parties that were different."

Silito looked coldly at Scooper and Gammon.

"You see the problem we have is Duncan Mule, Roger Thorndyke and Alec Blake had clearly been involved in these type of parties. Were they held at your property?"

"No comment."

This interview was following the same course as the one with Annie Frokel.

THE SORROW BEGINS

"Come on Maggie, I know you know something."

Maggie Silito just looked away.

"Do you know Annie Frokel?"

"No comment."

"You are really testing my patience Maggie, help yourself."

Again Maggie just looked at them in a cold manner.

"I think you have been got at. I also think you know more about these murders, am I correct?"

"No comment."

"Ok Maggie, your persistence in not helping this inquiry may, if proven, have consequences for you, maybe even deportation. Am I clear?"

John Gammon Peak District Detective

This seemed to make Maggie Silito smile as if she was untouchable. Gammon turned to Milton.

"Interview complete. You may leave Miss Silito, but may be asked back at any time during our on-going investigations."

Silito left.

"This is just ridiculous. In my mind whoever killed these men either were part of this syndicate which seems very dark to me, or it's something to do with Phil Sterndale."

"I agree John."

"Creep Milton. I don't John."

"Why creep, Sandra?"

"Only joking with Carl, John."

"So, who do you think did these crimes?"

THE SORROW BEGINS

"I truly don't have a clue. I think for the first time in my professional career nothing seems to add up John."

"Well I am sure DCI Cook is under pressure from above. It seems like we don't have anything."

Gammon left Milton and Scooper discussing it and Gammon filled in DCI Cook on the interviews. He went to his office feeling somewhat deflated. Sandra was right, he was clutching at straws. Gammon stood looking at Losehill from his office window hoping for some small clue to burst into his head.

There was a knock on his door. It was Sergeant Magic.

"Nipping into town Sir. Do you want a sandwich picking up?"

John Gammon Peak District Detective

"Oh thanks Magic, I'll have a chicken pasta salad please mate," and John passed Magic a new crisp five-pound note.

Twenty minutes passed and Gammon was still staring at Losehill when Magic arrived with his lunch. Gammon thanked Magic and sat with his pasta chicken and a coffee. He really wasn't hungry, and pushed his pasta round and round before finally picking it up and putting it in the waste bin. Gammon sipped his coffee and looked at his notes he had made earlier hoping for some inspiration, but nothing was coming through.

John called Saron and she sounded very happy which lifted John' spirits. Saron asked John to come to the Tow'd Man when he finished, which John agreed.

THE SORROW BEGINS

CHAPTER ELEVEN

It was 5.10pm when John left Bixton. As he got in his car his phone rang.

"Hello DI Gammon speaking."

The voice just said, "Meet me at the White Fox in Driffield in twenty minutes," and the phone went dead. Gammon was intrigued so set off for Driffield.

Driffield was on the outskirts of Derby. A pleasant village which housed a lot of upper class houses and was used as an easy commute to Derby and London. The three pubs were very up-market which included The White Fox, a bistro type pub. John had been in once some years ago, but it had a total refurbishment since then. John ordered a pint of Timothy Taylor's best bitter and sat down waiting for who, he didn't know.

John Gammon Peak District Detective

It wasn't long before a big man in a suit came and sat with Gammon.

"Mr Gammon I believe?"

"Are you the man who called me?"

"Yes I am, my name is Hurtful."

"Hurtful?"

Just then a man Gammon recognised instantly arrived at the table.

"Lund, what the hell?"

"Hold it there Johnny boy, don't be so excitable."

"What do you want, Lund?"

"Let's say a chat."

"I have no need to chat with you."

"Oh, but I think you do. You see I have some info that may help you."

"What do you mean help? Help with what?"

THE SORROW BEGINS

"Your latest case that I hear you are struggling with."

"Look Lund, I don't know how the hell you have escaped death and prison and I really don't want to know. Know this though Lund, I hate you with every part of my body and one day I will put you away, that I do promise you."

Gammon got up to walk away. Hurtful stood up and told John to sit down. He towered over John by a good six inches and had a scar across his face which made him look even more intimidating. Gammon looked at him.

"Move out of my way or you can pick a window, big lad."

Lund gestured to Hurtful to back off. Gammon brushed past Hurtful and headed for his car. Under the windscreen was a

John Gammon Peak District Detective

business card. It said Brian Lund and Associates. On the back was a hand-written note it simply said 'ring when you have run out of ideas.'

John was fuming. Lund was back in his life. John felt so annoyed he drove home and was halfway through a bottle of Jameson's when Saron rang.

"Where the hell are you? It's almost 9.00pm.

"Sorry Saron, I am home."

"Are you ok?"

"Think I have started with a bad cold."

John knew he was lying but he felt weak that Lund had walked back into his life.

"Ok sweetheart, I'll call you tomorrow. Get in bed and sweat it out."

THE SORROW BEGINS

Saron rang off. John felt guilty but seeing Lund had brought back all the carnage the man had caused, not least with his family. John polished the bottle off before climbing the stairs to bed.

Almost a week passed with still no movement on the murders. DI Cook asked to see Gammon.

"Where are we John? We seem to be stood still."

Gammon realised he had to tell Amanda about Lund. He showed her the card.

"So, he arranged to see you?"

"Yes, I met him at the White Fox in Driffield."

"Bit posh for Lund, isn't it?"

"He looked different Amanda. He has lost weight and was dressed in a suit."

John Gammon Peak District Detective

"So, what happened?"

"He was trying to tempt me. He was saying he could help."

"So, what did you say?"

"What do you think, Amanda?"

"This man tried to ruin my life. He created all the carnage with all those people losing their lives, and my family being part of it all."

"I know what you are saying John, but maybe we need some help."

"Not from him Amanda, we don't."

"John, we have to think out of the box. We are going nowhere fast at the minute."

"If you are suggesting, sorry telling, me to get back in contact with Lund you can have my warrant card first. Is there anything else Amanda?"

THE SORROW BEGINS

Gammon walked out, went straight to the coffee machine and went back to his office fuming inside. He knew Amanda is under pressure to get these murders solved, but there was no way he was getting help from Brain Lund.

With just over a week to Christmas and his wedding, John thought what the hell, maybe he should take a fortnight off and have a proper honeymoon? After half an hour he had calmed down, and knew until these murders were sorted any extended holiday wasn't going to happen.

The day petered out and John called it a night, and headed to see Saron. He headed through the back way to the Tow'd Man and into the kitchen. Saron was busy.

"Evening sweetheart."

John Gammon Peak District Detective

"Hey John, this time next week it will be Christmas Eve just before our big day. Are you nervous?"

"No, but you know I don't like ceremony, so will be pleased when we are married."

"I know John but the family I am from is full of pageantry."

"How many are coming?"

"Mum said in total four hundred and eighty two."

"Flippin' heck Saron, is your mum sure she hasn't missed anyone?"

Saron laughed showing her beautiful white teeth.

"Look, I have tried to keep you away from all the wedding stuff but we do have to see the vicar at Trissington church

THE SORROW BEGINS

tomorrow night, and you do have to be there, John."

"Ok, you win."

"What time?"

"7.00pm sweetheart, I will pick you up at 6.30pm."

"Forgot to say, did you mum order the snow for our wedding?"

"Now, now Mr Gammon, sarcasm doesn't suit you."

John smiled.

"Look sweetheart, I had enough drink during the stag do, so do you mind if I go home. I have a few bits to do."

"No problem sweetie. I'll see you tomorrow night."

"Oh, forgot to say, is Whitby ok? I have booked Christmas Day night and Boxing Day. Is that ok?"

John Gammon Peak District Detective

"That's fine sweetheart."

"We will have a proper honeymoon once I have cleared these murder cases up."

John kissed Saron and left for home.

The cottage was lovely and clean. Phyllis had been and cleaned and changed his sheets. He quickly showered and got in the bed. There was no other feeling as good as clean white cold crisp sheets. John was soon in the land of nod. He slept so well it was the alarm that woke him.

John showered and dressed and decided to call in at Beryl's Baps on the way in. The café although it had changed hands still had the mix of punters. Lorry drivers, factory workers from the brick works, and the office staff. John ordered a door-step bacon

THE SORROW BEGINS

and egg sandwich and a black coffee. There were very few greasy spoons that could compete with Beryl's. John finished and paid, then headed into work.

"Morning Sir."

"Yes, good morning Sergeant Yap, everything ok?"

"Yes, I think so Sir. No problems from last night, nothing reported Sir."

"Ok thanks Ian," and John climbed the stairs grabbing a coffee on the way. He had just got in his office when DCI Cook came in.

"Have we calmed down?"

"Well if you mean will I work with that scumbag Lund, the answer is still the same, not a chance."

John Gammon Peak District Detective

"Ok John, I was contacted by the Home Secretary, Sir John Banks, last night. I have to go to London for a few days."

"What, on account of me not working with Lund?"

"He didn't say John, so I don't know."

"Oh, come on Amanda, we know what it's about."

"Look John, don't take our friendship as a sign of weakness on my side."

"I'm sorry Amanda."

"You have no need to apologise John. I have misunderstood how much this man hurt you and your family, forgive me."

"Not a problem Amanda, would you mind if I crack on please."

THE SORROW BEGINS

"Ok John, I am leaving for London in half an hour, I will let you know the outcome."

Amanda left and John got up to get another coffee, but had to sit down quickly. The pain in his back was horrendous, he knew he had to make a decision once the wedding was over. He sat for almost half an hour before the pain subsided. Dave Smarty came in.

"You ok John?"

"Yes, fine Dave, why?"

"Just you look a bit pale."

"It's this lodged bullet. I am going to speak with Saron after the wedding. I think I am going to have to take my chance Dave."

"Big decision mate, have they said what the chances are?"

John Gammon Peak District Detective

"Sixty-forty."

"What sixty you will be ok?"

"No mate, sixty I will be paralysed, forty I will be ok."

"Oh, wow mate, didn't realise things might be that bad."

"It could happen anytime Dave, the bullet is so close to my spinal cord, a quick turn could render me paralysed."

"See what you mean, I never realised John, you never said."

"What will be will be Dave?"

"Ok, well on a lighter note in a couple of days it's Christmas Eve and we are all meeting for a drink. Amanda is putting some food on at the Spinning Jenny, just wanted to check you were coming."

THE SORROW BEGINS

"Will do mate, but can't be too late, it's my wedding day the next day."

"Understand mate. She has arranged for 4.00pm which is good of her."

"Yeah, think we at last have a good DCI, Dave."

"Can't think of a better one, other than you mate."

"Well don't think you will ever see that at Bixton mate. I have upset too many people."

"I heard you had turned down the job in London."

"Who told you about that?"

"Still got some mates down in the big city mate."

"Anyway Dave, I best crack on, loads to get through, and then having a couple of

John Gammon Peak District Detective

days off in Whitby. I best get my house in order mate."

"Ok John, pleased you are coming Christmas Eve mate."

John trawled through his paperwork. Just before he finished he phoned Steve and arranged to call on his way home.

John left Bixton, it was 6.20pm as John set off to see Steve. It was about twenty minutes from Bixton and John pulled into the sweeping driveway. The house looked magnificent. He rang the bell which sounded to Ian Drury's 'Hit me with your Rhythm Stick'. This always made John chuckle.

"Hey mate, come in Jo has made some dinner, come through."

THE SORROW BEGINS

The whole house was stunning. Steve showed John into the kitchen. Jo gave him a kiss. She had made chili con carne for the three of them.

"Hey this is really good of you Jo."

"Not a problem, we were eating anyway."

"So mate, what time Christmas Day?"

"I will pick you up at 12.30pm. We can have a couple on the way, then head for St John's church at Trissington."

"Oh John, I am so excited for you, well we both are. I still can't believe John Gammon is getting married again."

"Steve!"

"He is ok Jo, I can't believe it either," and he laughed.

John Gammon Peak District Detective

"What a wonderful setting it is John. What a shame her dad won't be there to see her."

"Well Jo he wasn't my favourite person, but I agree a father should see his daughter get married."

It was 9.30pm when John left thanking Jo and Steve for a nice evening. He decided to get straight home. John slept well.

It was soon Christmas Eve and John told Saron that he was finishing early to have a drink with the lads. She was at Trissington Hall and said it was bad luck to see him before the big day.

"Just don't go over the top John, you have a heavy day tomorrow."

"I know, don't worry I won't be silly."

THE SORROW BEGINS

"Love you, see you tomorrow John Gammon."

"Love you too lady, see you tomorrow."

John set off for work but called at a small bakery in Bixton and bought some mince pies to take in.

"Morning Sir."

"Morning Ian, please stick these on the front desk for everyone."

"Oh great, thank you Sir."

The station was generally a nice place to be on Christmas Eve with everyone smiling and sharing small presents for each other. John climbed the stairs to his office, meeting DCI Cook outside her office.

"You got a minute John?"

Amanda Cook was in a somber mood.

John Gammon Peak District Detective

"Take it the London trip didn't go well?"

"You can say that again John."

"So what happened?"

"Well first of all they are mightly pissed of that you turned their job down."

"Well they can't blame you for that."

"Then they kicked off at our perceived lack of progress in the murders, which they then turned round on me."

"You, why? We are all in this together."

"John, the buck stops with me."

"I fully understand that. This is just because I turned the pompous gits down, they are getting back at me through you."

Amanda had a tear roll down her cheek.

THE SORROW BEGINS

"Hey come on, we will find the murderer, stay positive," and John handed her an handkerchief.

"I'm ok John, let's not ruin the day or your day tomorrow."

John left and went to his office. Several of his colleagues dropped in either with a mince pie or a chocolate. It was soon 3.30pm and everyone started to head for the Spinning Jenny. The team deserved to finish early after the year they had. John was almost last to leave. Di Trimble had come on early to let Ian Yap go to the break up day.

When John arrived the food was just coming out. Carl Milton had a Santa hat on as did David Magic and Dave Smarty. Sandra Scooper looked well. Behind the bar was Tracey Rodgers and Anouska Sutra. DI

John Gammon Peak District Detective

Lee was talking to Anouska, clearly under her spell. She had a short denim mini skirt with a white blouse open revealing black underwear. John noticed Carl Milton watching anybody chatting to her.

It made a nice afternoon. By 9.00pm Anouska had come from behind the bar. Carl had gone home as he was very drunk. There was only John, Dave Smarty and DI Lee, but his taxi had just come. Anouska came over talking to John and Dave. By 10.30pm Dave had left and John decided he was calling it a night. The shock was to come, as John climbed in his car there was a knocking on the passenger door. It was Anouska.

THE SORROW BEGINS

"Can I come for a coffee to yours?" she said in broken English. Now was the test, could John resist? He thought for a second.

"By all means," he said. "Jump in."

Anouska was a very pretty girl and John was having all on concentrating. They arrived at the cottage.

"How pretty," she said in broken English.

"Come in, what would you like to drink?"

"Same as you please."

John poured two large Jameson's and he put some music on.

"Do you like music Anouska?"

"I like to dance," she said seductively grabbing John to dance with her. One thing led to another and before he knew what had happened they were both naked and

John Gammon Peak District Detective

romping on the settee. John hadn't had time to think about how wrong he was, so he just got on with it.

They made love another two times in bed. Sadly John didn't feel guilty as he lay with Anouska. The curtains were open and it was bright clear night. The stars were like a carpet of diamonds twinkling in the sky.

The following morning they both woke up at the same time, 9.10am.

"Anouska, I am so sorry, I get married today."

"I know John, but I have wanted you since I first saw you. I feel no guilt."

"You must never tell anybody Anouska."

THE SORROW BEGINS

"Of course I won't, I hope you are very happy with your woman, John?"

"Thank you. Come on let's have some breakfast."

"Are you at work today?"

"No, Kev shut the pub with going to your wedding."

"Oh, if that's ok will drop you off on my way to pick Steve up."

"Yes, that will be good John."

"Would you mind if I dropped you on the road though."

"No, that will be fine Mr Cautious."

They finished breakfast and John got himself ready for the wedding. When he came downstairs Anouska was smiling.

"What?" John said.

"Nothing, I was just thinking what a lucky lady she must be, John."

John Gammon Peak District Detective

John dropped Anouska at Blind Lane, about a third of a mile from the Spinning Jenny and headed off to pick Steve up. It was 12.20pm and he was almost at Steve's when his mobile rang. He didn't recognise the number.

"She is waiting for you," the voice said. "Go to the Old Candle Works in Cowdale, she wants to speak to you."

"Who does?"

The caller hung up. John called Steve.

"Look mate, just took an urgent call, got something to attend to. Go with Jo on the bus and I will see you in the Wop and Take pub at Trissington mate. Can't explain, see you there."

John carried onto Cowdale unsure of what the hell was happening. He finally

THE SORROW BEGINS

drove down the icy cobbled road towards the old candle factory which had been stood empty for as long as he could remember.

"Hello, hello," he hollered. He could hear something so advanced into the old building which was creaking. Parts of the roof were missing. In the main part of the building there was a small wooden set of steps that led up into another area. John looked at his watch it was now 1.00pm as he climbed the old wooden stairs. John was thinking of all the child labour that would have been used by the candle makers. The building was rusty and covered in cobwebs. John shoved the door open slightly ripping his coat in the process. Damn he thought, but it was nothing to the horror he saw. At the far side of the room was Annie Frokel tied up and covered in blood. He raced over

John Gammon Peak District Detective

to her but it was too late, she was dead. She had made a vain attempt at writing something in blood but it wasn't legible. John called the station and the ambulance, but he did explain the victim was dead. Speaking with Di Trimble he asked she give it major priority, as it was getting close to his wedding time. She assured John she would be quick and true to her word a DI Truman from Micklock Police came. He seemed to be light hearted saying it was a bummer that Micklock had to sort murders out for Bixton, because they were all at a wedding. John knew he didn't know it was his wedding. He filled him on the call he had, and said he would come in and make a full statement.

THE SORROW BEGINS

Now it was 1.38pm and John was a good twenty five minutes from Trissington. As he left Cowdale and poor Annie Frokel it began to snow. John's back was really hurting but he had to get going. He decided to drop down the valley hoping that would take a few minutes off the time. Luckily with it being Christmas there was nothing on the A roads and certainly nothing on the little B roads. John hadn't had time to get the Freelander out and the Jaguar wasn't great in the snow. He hadn't got much further to go and it was now almost 2.00pm. As he went around a sharp bend the snow was quite deep. It must have been snowing near Trissington longer than Cowdale. Suddenly the Jaguar's back end slipped and before John knew it he was off the road heading down a banking. The car flipped,

John Gammon Peak District Detective

hitting a tree before ending in a brook at the bottom. John was travelling in and out of consciousness unable to move his legs, the steering wheel was trapping him in.

Steve was pacing up and down. He had rung John ten times with no reply. Where the hell was he? He decided to walk up to the hall. It was snowing heavily. As he passed the small Trissington library Saron came by.

"Steve, where is John."

He didn't want her to panic so he said he was a couple of minutes behind him, and to go around the village again.

Steve was hoping John had gone straight to the little church. Steve climbed the steps to the church and went in. Of

THE SORROW BEGINS

course four or five of John's colleagues wanted to know where he was.

"I don't know, he said he would see me in the Wop and Take."

It was almost 4.00pm when Saron burst into the church in tears.

"It's off, why was I so stupid? Why did I think I could change him? All go home," she screamed.

Jo rushed to comfort her but she shrugged her off.

With John's marriage now off and the weather getting worse there was little chance of anybody finding him. John would be lucky if he was still alive in twenty four hours. The cold was biting through him. He could hardly breathe because of the steering

John Gammon Peak District Detective

wheel and most of the time he wasn't conscious.

THE SORROW BEGINS

If you have read the John Gammon books why not visit the Peak District and see the fictitious places loosely based in this beautiful place.

See if you can guess the villagers of Swinster and Hittington. Also the beautiful towns of Bixton, Ackbourne and Micklock. Why not find the pubs that John and his friends frequent. The Spinning Jenny, The Towd'Man, Up The Steps Maggie's see if you can guess where these pubs are loosely based on. You never know the characters might even be in there having a drink.

C J Galtrey.

Printed in Poland
by Amazon Fulfillment
Poland Sp. z o.o., Wrocław